# Crazy in Love

## Cheryl Thomas

ISBN: 979-8-9985365-4-0

# Chapter One

"I *do. I* do. I—do." I smile at myself in the mirror and practice the two simple, mundane words that are about to change my life forever. Until this moment, I have been the loner, the outcast, the eerily quiet one who no one notices. Invisible. But Cameron sees me. He is talented, popular, outgoing—loved by all. He could have anyone. Yet, he is choosing me.

"Your plain face doesn't matter." I hear him in my memory as clearly as if he is standing right next to me. As if it is happening again, right now. "I don't even mind the extra pounds," he says as he pinches my waist, squeezing half an inch of flesh between his fingers. It doesn't hurt much. And he is right. My mother always said that if you could pinch an inch, you needed to lose weight. I'm almost there. I will need to be careful.

The wedding planner—I think her name is Margot— zips up my dress and gives me a kiss on the cheek. She smells like lavender and mothballs.

"You look lovely, my dear," she says. I know she is lying, but I appreciate her attempt to make this day special for me.

Or for Cameron. I'm not sure, but I think she may be in love with him herself. Most sixty-something ladies are. They can't help it. When he turns on the charm, women of all ages are helpless.

"Thank you," I whisper shyly. I look in the mirror again and hardly recognize the woman standing there. *I do look lovely,* I allow myself to think for just a moment. The white lace compliments my tanned skin. My long, thick, brown hair falls loosely around my shoulders. Wavy curls hang in just the right places to accent my high cheek bones, flushed pink with excitement.

"Oh, I almost forgot," Margot says, picking up a small jewelry box from the table. "Cameron said to make sure you wear this." She opens the box and takes out a gaudy diamond necklace. "He rented it from Tiffany's. He wants everyone to know how much he loves you."

"But..." I finger the simple pearls I am already wearing. "These were my mother's. I really wanted to wear them."

"Nonsense, my dear. The diamonds are much prettier and go better with your gown. Here, let me help you." Her lips are turned down in a stern scowl, accenting the frown lines around her eyes and mouth.

Margot steps behind me and unclasps the pearls. I hang on to them. I know I should let go, but I just can't. I want my mother with me, but she is dead. This necklace is all I have of her. Margot gives a tug and the strand breaks, sending pearls flying. They roll everywhere—under chairs, behind the radiator, down the cracks between the floor boards. I watch, not moving, as if I am observing a terrible thing happening to someone else. My fist tightens around the few pearls still in my hand. I am grateful Margot cannot see the rage inside of me. I keep it hidden where it can do no harm.

"There, there. We'll have the janitor pick them up. I'm

sure Cameron will have the necklace fixed for you since it means so much." Margot kicks a pearl that has rolled next to her feet and sends it rolling toward the wall. She does not care.

"Okay," I say. I always say okay. No matter what I'm feeling, I have to be good. I'm afraid Cameron will not love me if I am disagreeable. Margot fastens the diamond necklace around my neck.

I hear the organ music start. Margot takes my arm and walks me to the door of the church sanctuary. She straightens my train and my veil and then gives me a little push. There is a pause as the organist turns the page of her music to begin the wedding march. Everyone turns around to get a glimpse of the bride and I hear their whispers and sighs. The bride. Me. I cannot seem to move.

"It's time," Margot says, wiping away a tear. "Oh, how I love weddings! Go on, dear. Everyone is waiting." She gives me another push. Just a small one. But, it is enough.

I walk slowly down the aisle, just like we rehearsed, my eyes focused on Cameron's face. I can't look anywhere else. He winks in that quirky way he knows I cannot resist, and I smile. Cameron holds out a hand as if he can't wait for me to be beside him. I am trying very hard not to run to him. The people in the pews are staring at me, and it is making me nervous. What I really want is to hide my face against Cameron's broad chest, to have him hold me, to protect me, to make the rest of the world disappear so that it's only us. I push away my feelings and finish the walk to the altar, taking his hand.

We turn toward the minister. I'm grateful Cameron doesn't let go. He knows me. He knows I need him. Desperately. He is my knight in shining armor, my protector, my confidant, my friend, my lover.

"Do you, Amelia, take this man to be your lawfully wedded husband?" The minister's voice sounds as if it is far away.

"I do," I whisper.

"And do you, Cameron, take this woman to be your lawfully wedded wife?"

"I do," he says, looking at me with so much love that it makes my heart skip a beat. It's not his slightly crooked nose I love, or his tightly curled hair, or that he is strong enough to carry me over his shoulder, or even his musical talent and the way he sings to me. It is his eyes that make me melt with desire.

He leans down to kiss me. I am embarrassed, but I try not to let it show. He would not like that. It's not that I'm embarrassed about kissing him. I enjoy kissing him. I'm embarrassed about kissing him in public. But Cameron doesn't agree with me about keeping our physical relationship private. In fact, he likes it when people see him kissing me or holding my hand or putting his arm around me. He seems almost proud about it, like he's some sort of conquering hero.

I can't think about that right now. I don't turn my head away as he leans down and I see the delight in his grin. I close my eyes and let him kiss me on the mouth.

The guests clap as we turn to walk back down the aisle and the minister announces us as Mr. and Mrs. Cameron Dallas, husband and wife.

I turn the name over in my mind. *Amelia Dallas. Amelia Nicole Dallas. Mrs. Cameron Dallas.* It feels a little like losing myself, the person I have been for twenty years, but I'm okay with the trade. Just five minutes ago, I was Amelia Alloway. Now, I am Amelia Dallas.

I have always hated the name *Alloway*. First, because it

belonged to my father, who I hardly ever saw. Second, because the boys in my high school would gang up on me in the hallway and ask me if I would go "all-o-way" with them. I can still see it clearly. They surround me like a pack of wolves stalking a fawn who has been separated from her mother. I try to avoid them, but the halls are crowded and the teachers are never around to see them grabbing my breasts or pinching my bottom. I learn to hold my books in front of me and walk sideways along the lockers, hair unkempt and hanging over my face as if it will hide me. If I can't see them, maybe they won't see me. But they imitate me and laugh. Even the girls snicker and point at me. Eventually, though, they all forget about me, and the torture stops. My mother says it is just normal, stupid, high school behavior and that it will stop in time. In time, just before graduation, it did.

Another memory stirs and I cannot escape the prison my mind has created. I see my mother coming to the graduation ceremony. She is too late, but she comes. My father forgets me, his only child. I look for them as I walk across the stage to receive my diploma. Everyone sees the disappointment on my face, and I hear the snickers as I walk past my classmates. "Even her parents hate her," I hear them say. I try not to cry. My smile is not fooling anyone.

The principal gives me a hug as she hands me my diploma. "It will be better in college," she says. "Hang in there."

She is right. I met Cameron at college.

I feel Cameron take my elbow. It is enough to bring me back to the present. He helps me into the limousine. I have no recollection of the receiving line, or of people throwing rice as we exited the church, although that must be what has happened, since Cameron is picking rice out of my hair as we settle into the back of the limo. I have been lost in my thoughts again. His dark eyes are flashing with anger. He pulls a strand of my hair out along with the rice. It hurts.

"I had to cover for you. You just stood there and stared into space. People were congratulating us and you didn't even acknowledge them. What is wrong with you? This is our wedding day and you are ruining it."

"I'm sorry, Cameron," I say. And I truly am sorry. "I don't know what happens. When things get overwhelming, I just...disappear. In my mind, I mean. And you know that I'm shy. I don't ever know what to say."

"How about a simple 'thank you'? Do you think you might be able to say that?"

I nod, afraid to make him any angrier than he is at this moment. "I'm sorry," I repeat myself. The tears well up in my eyes. He looks away, but doesn't release my hand. He squeezes it just a little harder than is necessary for reassurance, but I tell myself that is what it is. He is reassuring me that things will be okay, that they will be better now that he is with me. I try to squeeze back, but I can't. His grip is too tight. My fingertips are blue.

We arrive at the park where the photographer is waiting for us. Cameron lets go of my hand as he slides out of the car. I follow him to the small wooden bridge where we will stand for our first pose. There are willow trees and a cherry tree in full bloom behind it. A small waterfall to the left of the bridge completes the picture. It is breathtakingly beautiful. I stand next to Cameron on the bridge, unsure of what to do. The photographer barks out orders, and I follow them.

"Gaze into each other's eyes. Yes. Yes. That's good. Now, kiss. Now, put your head on his shoulder. Wrap your arm around her waist. Kiss her hand—the one with the ring on it. Pick her up over your head. Wow. That's great! Once more. Perfect. Perfect."

There's more, but I feel my mind retreating. *Stop. Stop it.* I imitate my mother's voice in my head. It works. Cameron is smiling, so I smile.

"Amazing!" says the photographer. The shutter clicks and clicks and clicks as Cameron and I walk together under the trees toward the waterfall. He holds my hand again, but he is gentle now, loving. He swings me around and dips me as if we are dancing. The photographer is delighted. Click. Click. Click.

"Where are the parents? Can we get some family photos?" the photographer asks.

I freeze. I have no one.

Cameron laughs. "Her parents are dead and buried," he explains to the photographer. "It would be pretty awesome to have them in the pictures, though. Maybe you can photoshop in ghostly auras or something."

The shock must show on my face. "I'm just kidding, Amelia," he says to me. "Lighten up. Here come my parents." Cameron leaves me standing under a willow tree and hurries over to be with his parents who are waiting at the opposite end of the bridge, watching us. The photographer follows Cameron and takes candid shots of the three of them. His younger brother, Mac, joins them.

"Shall we take a photo with Amelia?" Cameron's mother finally says.

"Oh!" The photographer looks around as if he is not quite sure who I am.

"Sure," Cameron says, beckoning to me.

I walk over and stand on his left side. Cameron's parents, Lorna and Laurence, are on his right. Mac takes his place on my right, so that I am between him and his family.

Cameron is in the middle, center stage, with his arm draped over his father's shoulders. That is exactly how he likes it. He enjoys the limelight. I much prefer the background or, even better, the edges of the background. I've gotten used to being unnoticed. It's comfortable. It's the only place I really feel like myself.

Laurence throws his car keys to Mac. "See you later, son," he says. "Be careful with my car." Mac grins and jogs off toward the parking lot.

Lorna, and Laurence join Cameron and me in the limo for the ride to the reception. They chatter happily with Cameron as I listen, nodding and smiling at all the right times. I can tell I am doing it right because Cameron is patting my hand and looking at me with approval.

My father set aside some money for my wedding before he died, but was not much. The reception is small. I have an aunt and some cousins who made the trip. I think they feel sorry for me, but I am still glad they are here. They fill up one table. Cameron's family fills up the rest of the room. Aunts, uncles, cousins, and friends. They are all here. I hear them complaining about the hall, about the food, about the decorations, about the music, about everything.

*"You think she could have done a little better than this..."*

*"I can't believe we have to pay for our own liquor."*

*"Well, you know she didn't want any alcohol served, but Cameron overruled her, thank goodness. At least we get wine for free."*

*"I can't get drunk on wine. What's a wedding without serious drinking?"*

Everyone at Laurence's table roars with laughter. They don't even try to hide their comments from me. It stings a little, but Cameron thinks it is funny. He has been drinking, too. I saw him at the bar with his friends. They were buying. They were generous.

"Where's Amelia?" I hear one of them say. I am standing right there, my back against the wall, watching the guests, watching Cameron, watching them. They remind me of the boys in high school. The drunker they get, the louder and more obnoxious they are. The dancing is getting wild, but, thankfully, no one grabs me and pulls me out to the middle of the dance floor.

I am happy they are having a good time, even if I am not. I am tired. I don't dare say anything to Cameron, though. The chance that he will be in a good mood later is greater if I don't remind him that I detest social activities of any kind, especially those that are supposed to center around me. Let this one center around Cameron. He enjoys it.

At one point, Cameron looks up from his dancing and sees me. He smiles and waves. I give a little wave back to let him know that I am fine. That was so sweet. My love for him swells and overflows onto my face. I smile and wipe away a happy tear. Cameron is having a good time without me, but he doesn't forget me. He knows. He understands me.

After what seems like an eternity, it is finally time to say good-bye to our guests and retire to the honeymoon suite upstairs. Cameron hugs everyone. I shake hands and allow a peck on the check from my new in-laws. I freeze the muscles of my face into a smile so they don't know how uncomfortable I am. They don't notice. They are drunk and well-fed.

Cameron and I run to the elevator and ride it to the top floor. The room is clean and large, although in need of renovation and updating. There is a bottle of champagne chilling in an ice bucket on the desk, compliments of the hotel.

I get ready first while Cameron sits on the bed and scrolls through his phone. He takes his turn in the bathroom as I lie alone on top of the worn bedspread in the dim light of the hotel room, waiting for him to finish brushing his teeth. I have on a white, lacy peignoir that I think is sexy and demure at the same time. I hope he will like it. He has seen me in pajamas, in nightgowns, in sweats, and even naked, but I want this night to be special so I have chosen to wear something he has never seen before. I hope the novelty and the sophistication of the negligee will mask my plainness and evoke the magical night I am imagining. It's my wedding night.

Cameron stubs his toe on the cabinet under the bathroom sink. I hear the thump. He swears as he opens the bathroom door, sending a flood of light into the room. He stumbles over to the bed and falls face-down.

"Shut off the lights," he says into the pillow I have plumped up and placed there for him.

I obey.

"Come here." Cameron pats a spot next to him on the mattress without lifting his head from where it lies buried in the pillow.

I follow the sound in the dark and find the bed, crawling up next to him. He reaches for me and finally looks up as his fingers tangle in the lace I am wearing.

"Take that off," he says.

"Do you like it?" I wonder how he can even see me in the dark.

"Not *on* you," he says. "Take it off."

He wants me naked. I could have saved $185.49. I wonder if Macys accepts returns of lingerie.

"Not yet." I am angry. "It makes me feel pretty. I want you to see it."

"Suit yourself," he says, rolling away from me.

I take it off and fold it neatly before crawling back into bed. I put my arms around him and snuggle against his back.

"That's more like it," he says, turning to face me.

"I'm sorry," I whisper, although I'm not sure what I am sorry about.

He runs his hands down my back and draws me close. I smell the alcohol on his breath as he kisses me, and I try not to pull away.

My mind wanders. *It's the only way I can do this tonight,* I think. It is our wedding night, though, and I do not dare to disappoint him, so I pretend to enjoy his sloppy, drunken lovemaking and instead think about the job I will be starting next week. I am looking forward to it. Accounting is my niche. I don't have to talk to people. Numbers are not as confusing as people. They are logical and always tell the truth.

One, two, three, four. I count his thrusts, knowing that it will be over when I get to fifty-two. He rarely goes beyond that, although if he slows down, there could be up to fourteen more than that.

*Fourteen.* That's how old I was the first time I ever saw a penis. I was at the mall, waiting with my friend Natalie for her mother to pick us up. The memory takes over and I feel like I am there again. We are sitting on the curb outside the back entrance. A man wearing a trench coat approaches us and asks for the time. Natalie is texting one of her many friends and cannot be bothered to answer him, but I start to look up and see that his pants are unzipped. He is holding his penis in his hand. It is long, pinkish-brown, and hangs limply between his legs. It almost reaches the tip of my nose as I look up. If I had not seen it, if I had tilted my head all the way back, it would have reached my lips. I turn away, stand up, and pull my friend to her feet.

"Let's go back into the mall," I tell her. "There is something I forgot to buy."

"What do you mean?" I can tell that she thinks he is handsome by the way she is smiling at him with her head tilted and her eyes wide open. He has his coat closed now. She did not see what I saw.

"Right now," I say more urgently. "Before your mom gets here. I really need it for school."

"What do you need?"

"Come on!" I pull her along with me and we go back into the mall. Once we are safely inside, I tell her what happened. She giggles.

"Let's not tell," she whispers. "My mom will never let us come here alone again if she knows." I think Natalie is planning to come back, to see for herself.

"No worries," I say. I do not want to ever speak of this again. It is disgusting. I get in the car and do not say another word all the way home. Natalie's mom drops me off at my house and I go inside.

My mother is there, on the floor, in the foyer at the bottom of the stairs. She is groaning. There is blood everywhere. It is hot and sticky. I hear the ambulance coming and am so scared I cannot breathe. The paramedics put her on the stretcher, assuring me she will be fine. They have arrived in time.

I see my father at the top of the stairs. He is angry, clenching and unclenching his fists at his sides. He looks at me and then walks back into his bedroom and shuts the door. My mother groans again and calls my name.

But, no. It is not my mother making those noises. I come back to the present. It is Cameron. *Fifty-one. Fifty-two.* He collapses on top of me. He is heavy. I cannot breathe. I wriggle out from underneath him and take a deep breath. He is asleep already. It's been a long, stressful day for him.

I feel sticky, thick liquid slowly running down my leg. I tiptoe to the bathroom and turn on the shower. I'm not crying. It's just the water from the shower head running over my face.

# Chapter Two

Cameron has been so busy with his band that I have hardly seen him since we've been home. The wedding was only two weeks ago, but it feels like such a long time. We are an old married couple already. I smile. I like that feeling. We are comfortable together. I cook breakfast for him on the weekends, but on the week-days he just buys an egg and cheese sandwich from the deli on his way to work. I think that is very thoughtful of him since we both leave for work at 7:30 and I need the time to make our lunches before we go. I do not stop for breakfast, though. I bring hot tea with me in a Styrofoam cup. No sugar. No cream. That is enough. I have to watch my weight. Cameron can tell if I gain even an ounce.

We put off our honeymoon until the fall. Cameron's schedule is so busy, he can't get away until then. His band plays for all of the society weddings. It's not really how he earns a living, but he would like it to be. I know he dreams of being rich and famous. I would like that for him too. For right now, though, he teaches piano at the Bach Academy of Musical Arts in Poughkeepsie during the day. I'm not sure who comes so early in the morning for piano lessons, but I suppose that is none of my business.

My job is in Garrison. I work at Roger Smithfield and Associates, Accountants and Tax Preparation and I have actually made a friend there with a woman named Jane. I've never had a friend before. Except for Cameron, of course.

"Call me Janey," she said when we met. "It makes me sound younger."

I laugh. She has wrinkles around her mouth and eyes as if she has been smiling every day of her life. Her gray hair is messy, and she tucks it behind her ears to keep it out of her face. We are quiet when we are working, but at lunch, we go to a picnic table in the courtyard, away from everyone else, and talk about everything.

"Tell me how you and Cameron met," she says one day.

"We met in college." I feel shy, talking about Cameron. I sometimes feel that he is a fantasy, someone I have made up, and who might disappear if I talk about him. But, no, he is real. I made his lunch this morning and kissed him good-bye as he went to work. I show Janey a picture of him on my phone.

"Hmmm," she says chewing her sandwich. "Not much to look at, is he? How did he land a beautiful girl like you?"

"Oh! I am not beautiful at all, but thank you for saying so, Janey. Cameron may not be the most handsome man on the planet, but he is a very talented musician. Everyone likes him because he's so outgoing and friendly. I am very lucky he chose me."

"Tell me about him," Janey says with furrowed brows. She's not convinced. I know she has noticed the finger-shaped bruises on my wrist this morning and is wondering how I got them.

"He is the first guy who has ever really seen me for me—

looked past my shyness and my awkwardness around people, you know." I shrug. "It all started when I fell down the stairs at the college on my way to the cafeteria. Everyone else just went around me, like I was just a chair or something in their way. Cameron, well, he actually stopped to ask if I was alright. When he saw that my head was bleeding, he helped me up and walked me to the nurse. She said I had to go to the hospital to get stitches and be checked out for a concussion. Cameron volunteered to drive me and he didn't even know me."

"That was nice." Janey's brows are a bit less furrowed.

"Yes, it really was! He waited at the hospital with me and then took me out for lunch afterward. He's very thoughtful like that. Kind. Generous."

"Uh huh," Janey says, her mouth full again.

"I almost fell again today and he grabbed my wrist to keep that from happening." I show her my wrist. "He saved me from another head injury. My brain can't afford another concussion! I have enough trouble with my memory already." I laugh and she laughs with me. I think she looks relieved. I don't tell her I made Cameron angry when I accidentally stumbled into him this morning or that he pulled me by the wrist down the stairs into the kitchen afterward. "You're not hurt," he had said, watching me rub my wrist.

"Cameron has been playing keyboard in a band since he was thirteen. He's very good. Much better than I am." I say to Janey instead.

"You play the piano?" Janey looks surprised.

"I used to," I admit. "And I sing, er, uh, used to sing."

"You did?" Janey raises an eyebrow.

"Yes. I was asked to perform at Carnegie Hall once, but turned it down." I don't know why I am telling her this. It just pops out of my mouth before I can stop it.

"You are full of surprises," Janey says. "Tell me more."

When I shake my head no and look away, embarrassed, she googles my name and clicks on link.

"Is this you?" She holds up an article on her phone about my junior vocal recital at college. The journalist raves about my technique and musicianship and predicts I will be a famous singer one day. I recognize the article right away. I have a copy saved in a tampon box in my closet.

"What happened? Why don't you sing anymore? Or play the piano?" she asks.

"Cameron didn't think I was very good at either. I would rather help him and support his career goals, like any good wife would, rather than chase my own, futile dreams."

"Didn't you like it? Singing, I mean." Janey is staring at me, her eyes intense. She seems determined to force the truth out of me, if necessary.

"Oh, yes. It was like I was a different person when I sang. I would just get lost in the music and forget there were people watching me. It was wonderful."

"And you gave that up?"

"For Cameron, yes, of course. I sometimes still sing when no one is around, just for fun, but I put away any thought of having a career in music. It's not as important to me as Cameron is. I want to do things that he approves of so he will be proud of me. Plus, it's very difficult to make any money as a performer. You have to be the best of the best. That will never be me, so why continue to chase that dream? I enjoy what I do now. I'm happy."

"Good for you." Janey pauses and looks like she wants to say more, but our timer goes off, and we head back to our desks in the Smithfield and Associates office building.

I glance over at her before unlocking my computer screen. She is sitting back in her chair, arms crossed. I see her check her watch and then shuffle through one of the stacks of paper on her desk. Her desk is as messy as her hair, but it doesn't slow her down. She's the most productive, most clever, most accurate accountant in the office. I want to be just like her someday.

# Chapter Three

It is now the end of September and the trees are brilliant shades of orange, red, and yellow. I want to go to Vermont for our honeymoon, but Cameron informs his parents that he has purchased cruise ship tickets to Jamaica. I tell him I would rather drive north and stay at a cute bed and breakfast inn, where we can snuggle together in front of a cozy, crackling fire as we talk for hours. He snorts as if I am joking and says, "The weather will be so much better in the Caribbean."

So, we board a plane to Miami, where we will meet the ship and enjoy time on warm beaches. I brought a bikini, even though I don't know if I will be brave enough to wear it.

Neither of us has ever been on a plane before. I hold Cameron's hand tightly, not caring that we are in public. The fear wins. He smiles at me. "This is fun," he says reassuringly. I nod, too nervous to speak. September is hurricane season in the Caribbean.

We find our seats. It is a short flight. Cameron laughs and jokes with the stewardess. I lean my head against the window and squeeze my eyes shut. I am terrified, but Cameron thinks I am sleeping. I hear him sigh and recline his seat.

The plane takes off, and we are in the air. I force my eyes open and look out the window. Below us are white, fluffy clouds. It's like we are angels, flying far above the earth without a care in the world. It's peaceful, really. I wonder if death is like this.

"Well, hello, sleepyhead," Cameron says to me.

"I'm sorry. I wasn't sleeping. I was just not looking."

Cameron laughs. "It's not so bad, is it?"

"No. Not at all," I say sitting up. "It's very peaceful. Can you see the clouds below us?"

Cameron leans over me and looks out the window. "Wow," he says. "Wow."

He pushes against me with his body in his effort to see outside the plane. It's hard for me to breathe, but I don't want to ruin this moment for him.

After a minute, he sits upright. "That is amazing."

"It's beautiful," I agree. I am not afraid anymore. We have shared a new experience that has both of us awestruck. I love him so much. I reach over and take his hand. Cameron looks surprised, but pleased. I leave my hand in his until the stewardess comes and asks what we would like to drink.

"Water for my wife, and a coke for me," Cameron says. He's so thoughtful. "She's watching her weight," he tells the stewardess, winking at her.

Embarrassed, I lean back against the window.

"Oh, don't pout," Cameron says. "I'm just joking."

The stewardess brings our drinks. Cameron turns on his most charming smile. He lets his hand brush against hers as he takes the can of coke she offers him. "Thanks," he says.

The stewardess smiles and glances at me briefly before she replies, "You're welcome. Let me know if you would like anything else."

"I will," Cameron says, raising his eyebrows suggestively. I see him wink at her again. She moves on to the people in the seat behind us.

Cameron seems so confident, but I know a different side of him. I know he is nervous about this trip. I can see it in the way he glances around, checking the signs to be sure we are in the right place. I see it in the way he constantly checks his watch, afraid that we will miss our cruise ship boarding time. I even see it in the way he walks, with long, brisk strides. After we debark from the plane, I hurry to catch up and struggle to stay one step behind him. I am confident that he will get us where we need to be. I have never doubted him. He has always taken care of me. It's what I love most about him.

It feels good to be cared for. Until I met Cameron, I had to take care of myself. My parents were always so busy and then, after my mother died, my father just forgot that I was there, I think. Or maybe I reminded him too much of her. I don't know. What I do know is that Cameron looks out for me in a way that no one has done before. I can't wait until we are in our stateroom on the ship so I can show him how much I appreciate that.

# Chapter Four

I thought there would be sex on a honeymoon. Cameron doesn't seem interested at all. Instead, we sit on the beach during our first port of call and he tells me he is not feeling well. He misses his parents, I think. He hasn't been away from home before. I thought wearing the bikini would help distract him, but he doesn't seem to notice. He lays on a towel while I romp in the ocean waves on the cruise company-owned, secluded section of the island. Nothing I say persuades him to join me.

"I hate the sand," he says, even though coming here was his idea. "It gets everywhere."

"Come in the ocean and wash it off," I say. He ignores me and picks up a book. "Please?" I urge him. "It's refreshing."

"No." He opens his book. Clearly, I am not enticing enough.

"Let's go into town, then. We can shop for souvenirs for your parents." I am hoping this will lift his mood. It seems to work a little. He hands me a towel and I dry off. I pull a coverup over my head and slip on my sandals. He puts his t-shirt back on and gives the towels back to the attendant.

"We have to be careful what we spend." He says *we* have to be careful, but I know he means me. But I am not a spendthrift. I buy nothing. I am just happy to look at everything. I have no money of my own anyway. My paycheck is deposited directly to a savings account that is only in his name. I am allowed to use our joint credit card to buy groceries and other necessities each week. I have what I need so that's fine with me. He's the man and that's the way it works best.

We stop at a street vendor's table, where Cameron purchases a straw bag with "Jamaica" embroidered on the front of it for his mother and a box of cigars for his father and brother.

When we board the plane for the return trip a few days later, Cameron is finally happy again. "Did you have a good time?" he asks me.

"Yes. Did you?"

"Of course. But it will be nice to be back home, don't you think? In our own bed, our own place, no sand everywhere."

I smile at him. "That will be nice." I do like having our own place.

I am not scared this time. The plane takes off in Miami and lands in New York, and I keep my eyes open the whole time.

"How was your trip?" Janey asks me at work the next day.

"It was fun." I smile brightly at her. At least, I hope it looks that way.

"So, tell me about it." She sits down and opens her lunch bag.

"Oh, not much to tell. Ocean, sand, warm temperatures. You know, the usual Caribbean stuff." I shrug.

She puts her sandwich down and looks at me. "Did you —um, *fall*—during your trip—and have to have Cameron *save* you?"

"Oh, no!" I am shocked at her accusatory tone. "Not even once."

"Good," she says, picking up her sandwich. "Good."

"How was work while I was gone?"

"Busy. The boss made me do your work. He said it couldn't wait."

"I'm sorry, Janey. I finished as much as I could before I left. They shouldn't have made you do that." I feel guilty.

Janey smiles. "It's okay. The overtime money will come in handy with Christmas only three months away."

I frown. Christmas. It has never been my favorite holiday. In fact, I never even knew it existed until I was five and in kindergarten in southern California. The other students were so excited about a person they called "Santa." I can still see them clearly: They are drawing pictures of a fat man with a white beard that covers his face. He is dressed in red with a wide belt that stretches across his plump belly and black boots that look like they might leave Sasquatch-size prints in the white fields that stretch across the landscape behind him. He has several animals that resemble very large deer, but they have multi-point horns like tree branches coming out of their heads. Evidently, they can fly, or so my best friend Caroline tells me in five-year old wonder, her eyes wide and sparkling. I wonder what has happened to Caroline. My family moved to New York when I was seven, and I never saw her again.

"What are you doing for Christmas this year?" Janey's question breaks into my thoughts.

"Oh, I don't know yet." I am embarrassed to tell her I am dreading the holiday. "Probably spending the day with Cameron's family."

"Have you started your shopping yet?"

"Shopping?"

"For presents, silly girl. Christmas presents."

"Oh, no. I haven't really thought about it yet."

"I can go with you if you want. I love to shop! There's a craft fair next weekend at the Civic Center. They always have unique things there that make great gifts."

"That sounds like fun, but I'll have to ask Cameron."

"Hmph." Janey grunts. She picks up her garbage and throws it away.

"Don't be so judgmental," I tell her. I am a little angry. I haven't gotten much rest the past week, and I am grouchy. "I have to consider Cameron's feelings. That's what being married means. I can't be independent and do whatever I want anymore."

"And neither can he, right?" Janey gives it right back to me.

"Of course not."

"He always checks in with you before he goes somewhere, or buys something, or makes plans? "Yes." I am lying. I think Janey can tell. She looks at me suspiciously and grunts again. I can't meet her eyes.

Our timer goes off. Time to go back to work. I am relieved.

# Chapter Five

"Where are you going?" I ask Cameron. It's 6:30 a.m. on Saturday, but he is up and already dressed in beige khakis and a navy blue polo shirt. His hair is combed and his face neatly shaven. He looks nice. I smell a hint of cologne.

"I'm going out for breakfast with a friend."

"Who?" I wonder which of his friends will be up this early. I push back the covers and get out of bed.

"You don't know her."

"Her?" I wonder if I should be angry. Why is he meeting a woman? I'm sure he has a good reason, though. He isn't cheating on me. He wouldn't do that. Would he?

"A friend from high school. We're just meeting for breakfast."

"Is anyone else coming?"

"No."

"Can I come? I'd like to meet her." I push the panic away. There's nothing to worry about. He said it was just a friend. He has lots of friends. Nothing at all to worry about. Is there?

26

"No." He grabs his jacket and heads for the door. "I'll be back later."

"Okay," I say.

When he is gone, I dial his father's number.

"Hello." Laurence is always up early. He sounds busy, like I've interrupted him.

"Hello," I say hesitantly.

"What is it?" He is impatient.

"Cameron went out for breakfast with a girl." I don't know why I am telling him.

"I'll take care of it," he says. He hangs up.

I stare at the phone in my hand. I don't know what Laurence will do. I don't care. I get dressed, make myself a cup of tea, and settle into a chair near the large living room window.

About an hour later I hear Cameron and Laurence arguing outside.

"You can't do that!" Laurence's voice is angry.

"Why not?" Cameron is calm.

"You're a married man now."

"So?"

"So you cannot go out with other women."

"Olivia is just a friend."

"Knock it off, Cameron."

"Or else?"

"You need to be faithful and attentive. Who knows? You might actually learn to love her. She's not bad looking, you know."

Cameron shrugs and glances toward the door. He speaks just a little louder, as if he knows I'm listening. "You're right, Dad. And I do love her. I won't do it again,"

"That's my boy," Laurence says, patting him on the shoulder. Laurence gets into his car and drives away.

Cameron opens the door and comes into the house. I am still sitting in the chair near the window. I don't get up. He comes to me and kneels down in front of the chair, putting his head in my lap.

"I'm sorry," he says. "Olivia is just a friend. There's nothing between us, but I know how it must look to you, though. I won't do it again."

"Thank you, Cameron," I say, stroking his hair. "That means a lot to me."

I trust him. It was foolish of me to have ever doubted his loyalty.

Cameron takes my hand off his head and sits up. He stares into my eyes. "Don't call my father again. Tattling is very unattractive. I don't like it."

"Oh," I say, startled. "I—uh—didn't mean to tattle. I just..."

"So, you see how *that* looks to me, don't you? We're not little kids who tattle on each other. We're adults. We're married. We need to have each other's backs, not try to get other people to see us as the bad person in the relationship. We should only be saying good things about each other."

"I'm sorry, Cameron." I don't know what else to say. He's right. I should be ashamed.

"If you don't like something I am doing, talk to *me*, babe. Not to my father or to your friends."

"Okay. I will." In the back of my mind, I briefly remember that I did try to talk to him and he ignored me. I don't bring that up.

"Let's drive to Vermont," he says.

"Now?" I say. "It's November and cold."

"Sure," he says, jumping to his feet. "We'll stay overnight. I'll find a bed and breakfast with a fireplace while you pack for us. We can go to the Vermont Teddy Bear Factory for a tour and maybe take a hike. It will be fun!"

It *will* be fun. I let myself feel the excitement. I will have Cameron to myself for two whole days.

We head out. It's only after an hour that I realize I forgot to pack my birth control pills. I don't dare tell him. I might not need them anyway. Cameron can go days without sex. I sometimes think that means he doesn't love me. If he loved me, he would want to touch me, hold me, kiss me. Instead, he usually just gets into bed, rolls over, and goes to sleep. Sometimes there is a kiss before he dozes off, but sometimes there is not. It's confusing.

Perhaps it's just that I don't know the rules. There must be rules. The world is orderly. The sun comes up and goes down each day. The seasons come and go the same way they have for thousands of years. People are born, and they die. Flies always find the leftover food left on the counter. A lemon is always sour. Relationships must also have rules. *If you make love to me, then you must love me.* It's even in the words.

Cameron is chatty today. I enjoy that. It means he is happy.

"I booked a place right on Lake Champlain." Cameron grins at me. "We were lucky they had a last-minute cancellation. It has a fireplace."

"That sounds nice. Romantic."

Cameron looks sideways at me. His eyes sparkle. "I hope so," he says. "I have something special planned for us."

"Tell me!" I urge him.

"Nope. It's a surprise."

"Should I be worried?"

"Not at all. You'll like it."

I am curious, but he changes the subject.

"Tell me about your past boyfriends," he says. "What were they like?"

"Oh, I had a few crushes when I was a teenager, but nothing amounted to much. I was too shy."

"Really? You never kissed a boy? Or a girl?"

"Cameron!"

He shrugs. "Just curious."

"Boys tried to kiss me in high school, but I'm pretty sure it was not because they liked me. I think they were daring each other to kiss the ugly girl just to make fun of me."

"You never wanted to kiss anyone?"

I hesitate for a moment. "Of course, I did, but he didn't want me, so..."

"What about me?" Cameron asks. "What made you want me?" He doesn't look at me. Instead, he studies the road ahead as if the answer to his question is not really all that important to him.

"You were kind to me. No one has ever been as kind or attentive to me as you are. You listen to me and understand me."

He looks at me with curiosity and smiles, so I continue.

"My parents were always too busy with their own lives to notice me most of the time. I felt invisible. They appreciated when I was quiet and stayed out of their way and out of trouble, I think. That was the most I could hope for—gratefulness instead of love or approval. It was hard for me to make friends. I never knew what to say or how to make conversation. I even looked up a book in the library once on how to hold a conversation."

"You did?" Cameron looks amused.

"It didn't help." I smile back. "But, you are so outgoing, I always know you will carry the conversation when we are out with your friends or around your family. It takes the pressure off of me, you know?"

Cameron nods. "I wish you would talk more, though," he says. "My friends think you are stuck-up."

That stings. I can't help the tears that threaten to spill from my eyes. "I'm not stuck-up at all! I have nothing to be stuck-up about!"

"I know that. Just talk more. Be friendly."

"I'll try." I want to please him.

"What about you?" I ask. "Did you have a lot of girl-friends?"

"No." Cameron's answer is terse, almost like he is embarrassed to admit it. "There was a girl in high school that let me feel her up, but she wasn't really my girlfriend. And there was an older woman who lived down the street that took my virginity." He sees my shocked reaction and grins. "Consensual, of course. She taught me a *lot*. Then, I dated a girl or two in college, but nothing serious until you."

"Really?" I am pleased.

"Really," he says, reaching over to take my hand.

My heart skips a beat. He does that to me. I think I must be the luckiest girl in the world.

# Chapter Six

The cabin is small and the furnishings are worn, but it is cozy. The other cabins around us are empty. It is the off-season between the tourists wanting to see the beautiful fall leaves and the skiers who come for the mountains and snow. We have complete privacy.

Cameron gathers wood from the shed in the back and builds a fire in the fireplace. It's late, and I am hungry and tired. I unpack the sandwiches I made for us and set them out on Melamine plates I found in a kitchen cabinet. Cameron picks his up and takes it to the overstuffed couch in front of the fireplace. I take a bite of my sandwich, then follow him to the couch. He pats the seat beside him.

"Come. Sit," he says through a mouthful of food.

I sit.

"Why did you make tuna?" he asks me. "I told you I wanted turkey."

"I'm pretty sure you said tuna," I tell him without thinking.

"No. I said turkey. Your kooky brain just mixed up the words since they both start with t."

I reach into my memory. I am sure he said tuna, but it really isn't something to argue about. "Sorry. If you are hungry, maybe we can send out for delivery."

"No. I'll eat this. It's fine. I already spent enough money on this cabin for you. We don't need to spend any more because you made a mistake. I always listen to you, but you can't seem to listen to me." Cameron is pouting, and I feel guilty. I think that I hang on to every word he says, but maybe it's true that I am not a good listener? I do sometimes retreat into my own world, but I'm sure this is not one of those times. That only happens when I'm nervous or afraid.

"How can I make it up to you?" I want him to have a good time. I want him to enjoy being with me.

Cameron finishes his sandwich and gets up to get another beer without saying a word. He's grumpy, and I don't know what he will do next. He keeps his back to me so I cannot see his face, but I get the impression he is smiling—but not a nice, happy smile. I imagine an unpleasant smile, a malevolent smile. It sends shivers down my spine. But, when he turns around to face me, there is no smile at all. His expression is blank. He reaches out a hand, and I go to him.

"Never mind," he says. "Come with me."

Cameron takes me into the bedroom. There is a large, four-poster bed against one wall, an overstuffed armchair under the window, and an old bureau near the door. An antique quilt covers the bed. I admire it for a moment, running my hand over it to feel the tiny, careful stitches.

"Undress," Cameron tells me. "I want you naked."

He wants me. I am relieved. He is not angry. He has forgiven me. He loves me.

While I take off my clothes, he reaches into the duffel bag he brought and pulls out four neckties.

"Lay on the bed."

I obey.

He raises my arms above my head and uses the neckties to fasten my wrists and ankles to the bedposts. I am helpless and exposed, and I shiver in the cold. He pulls one more item out of the duffel bag. It looks like a whip with a handle about a foot long and several dozen thin straps of leather on one end. Cameron runs the straps across my breasts and between my legs.

"Isn't this fun?" His voice is husky, breathless. His eyes are glassy and narrowed into slits as he runs the leather over my body and then hits me lightly with it.

I can't answer. I feel myself retreating, running back into my mind again. Flashes of memory break through. I am three years old, tied up and alone in a dark closet. I am four and hiding under my bed, watching the large brown dirty boots walking into my room, looking for me. I am eleven and being forced to lower my pants so my father can spank my bare bottom to punish me. I am twelve and an uncle is groping my breasts.

"You're so beautiful," Cameron whispers in my ear. His beer breath disgusts me, but I don't complain.

I fight the mental fog closing in on me and struggle against the ties holding me in place. "Wait! Wait, Cameron!"

But he doesn't wait. He mounts me, and I begin counting silently to calm the panic building inside of me. But it's really not that bad. He's not hurting me. I relax. He stops and smiles at me, head tilted to one side as if to ask my permission to continue. I smile back at him.

The next morning, Cameron takes me to visit the

Vermont Teddy Bear Factory. He sees one he knows I will like and buys it for me. It is a girl bear with golden brown fur, dressed in a green and red plaid dress. She holds a small notebook and pen and wears glasses. "Thank you," I tell him. This is just another way that he shows me how much he loves me, and I am truly grateful.

"Do *you* want anything?" I ask him, looking around the gift shop.

"Just you," he says, gazing into my eyes and smiling.

"You will always have me," I say, smiling back. And I mean it. I can't imagine my life without him. He is mostly kind. I know he slips up now and then, but all men do.

"Men have *needs*, Amelia," my mother explained to me when I was old enough to understand. "Needs that only we, as women, can meet. So, stop complaining and do what you're told. Be happy that you have been chosen. Not just *anyone* is chosen, you know."

Cameron is much, much better than the other men I have known. He actually loves me. I know he does. And I have never loved anyone the way I love him.

# Chapter Seven

I'm pregnant. I'm sure of it. It's the middle of December and I'm late. I am never late. I turn sideways and look at myself in the full-length mirror leaning up against the wall in my bedroom. The silky dress I am wearing clings to my body and shows off every curve. I run my hand over my belly. It is flat. *I wonder when I will show*, I think. I am embarrassed. People will know we had sex. Yes, of course, that is what married people do, but still... To have the evidence right in front of you, wherever you go, for all to see, and to have people imagining the things that happen in your bed—well, it's embarrassing. I decide not to tell anyone until I have to—not even Cameron. He will tell everyone. He will boast about how virile he is to have gotten me pregnant already.

"Hurry up!" Cameron shouts from the living room. "We'll be late."

"I can't find my shoes," I call back. I look under the bed and in the closet. I had not even taken them out of the box. They are brand new, bought just for tonight's party with

Cameron's work friends. I retrace my steps. I brought them home from the store in a bag, took them out of the bag, and put the box in the closet before throwing out the bag. I look in the wastebasket. The bag is there. I look in the closet again. The shoes are not there.

I go out into the living room. "I'm sorry, Cameron. I know I put them in the closet, but I can't find them."

He points to the kitchen. "Are you sure you didn't put them somewhere else, like on top of the refrigerator?"

I look. The shoebox is there. On top of the refrigerator.

"Geez, Amelia. Why would you put them there?"

"I—I didn't." I look back and forth between Cameron and the shoebox, confused.

"Well, they are there, aren't they? Who else would have done that?" He gets them down for me and I put them on. "Don't worry, darling. I won't tell anyone," he says. "Just hurry and get ready so we can go."

"I am ready," I tell him. "Thanks for finding my shoes. I don't know what I was thinking, putting them there." He locks the front door behind us as we walk down the steps to where he has parked the car in front of our house.

"No problem." Cameron opens the car door for me and we get in.

I am sure I did not put my shoes on top of the refrigerator. I am sure. I am—almost sure. Did I? I have never done anything like that before. I would have had to pull over the step stool and climb up to reach that far. Why wouldn't I remember doing that? It scares me.

Cameron looks over at me and sees the fear on my face. He misunderstands it. "Don't worry, Amelia. You won't have to say much at the party. I'll take care of you."

"Thank you, Cameron. I'll try my best, though."

"I know you will, darling," he reassures me.

Cameron's best friend, Eric, waves at us from across the room as we enter the restaurant.

"Over here!" He shows us the way to the room the restaurant has reserved for the party.

"Hi! I'm Lyla, Eric's girlfriend." A girl about my age with beautiful brown, curly hair and a warm smile gives me a hug. I don't pull away. I instantly like her. She is about my height, but curvier in all the right places. Her dress is a gorgeous shade of deep royal blue, matching the color of her eyes.

"Hi. I'm Amelia, Cameron's wife," I respond shyly.

"Come, sit next to me. We don't have to pretend we enjoy the guys' conversation that way!"

I follow her to a round table at the far end of the room. Cameron nods at me and winks before turning back to Eric. He throws an arm around Eric's shoulders and the two of them walk toward the bar.

"Those two are trouble when they get together." Lyla laughs as she pulls out a chair and sits down. There is a pitcher of water on the table. Lyla reaches for it and pours a drink for me and for herself. She takes a sip. "So, Amelia, what do you do? How did you meet Cameron? How long have you two been together? I have so many questions!"

"I'm an accountant. I met Cameron in college. We've been together a little over two years now, but married for only eight months." I am not sure what else she wants to know. I'm not good at making friends or holding conversations.

"Wow! An accountant! Beautiful *and* smart. I'm impressed. Cameron hit the jackpot with you, honey." She laughs, and I can't tell if she is joking.

"Oh, no. I'm the lucky one. I can't believe I'm his wife. I

have to pinch myself sometimes to make sure I'm not dreaming."

Lyla looks at me and shakes her head. "Seriously? I hope you always feel that way, but—never mind," she says.

"How long have you known Cameron?" I ask her.

"Oh, not long at all. I just hear tales from Eric. They've been best friends forever, I think." She takes another sip of water, almost as if she wants her mouth busy doing something besides talking about Cameron. "I met Eric in college, too. We were both in the teacher prep program."

"You're a teacher? I always thought that would be fun," I tell her. "I love children." My left palm rests protectively against my abdomen.

"I don't have a job yet, but I've applied everywhere. I guess elementary teachers are a dime-a-dozen. Eric found a job, though. He'll be working in Poughkeepsie as a social studies teacher in the high school. They want him to start right after the winter break in January. He's trying to get Cameron a job there, too. They need music teachers." Lyla pushes a strand of hair behind her ear and leans back in her chair. "As for me, I'm just doing a lot of substitute teaching right now, until something permanent comes along."

"Oh." I don't know what else to say so I just nod. That seems to encourage her and she keeps talking.

"I think Eric will propose once he gets settled in his job," she confides in me. "I think he's waiting to make sure he can support both of us on his teacher's salary." Her eyes sparkle, and I smile back at her. I know that feeling of hope, of anticipation that something wonderful is about to happen.

I glance over at Eric and Cameron. They are still at the bar, talking and laughing. "He seems like a good guy," I tell Lyla.

"Oh, he is!" I can see she wants to tell me all about him. "He takes care of me already. He lets me use his credit card and always makes sure I have everything I need. He even paid for braces for me." She smiles broadly and I can see she has perfectly straight, perfectly white teeth.

"That's nice," I tell her, and I mean it. I am happy for her.

"Oh, yes," she says. "They were very crooked before. I was embarrassed to smile. Eric never minded. He told me I was beautiful anyway and he didn't care, but because it made me so sad, he offered to help. He'd saved money for a trip to Germany but gave that up to be able to afford to pay for my braces. I love him so much for that. He's absolutely *perfect*." She says "perfect" like she's purring with pleasure.

No man is that selfless. I think she will learn that soon enough, but I don't say so out loud. Instead, I nod and smile and let her think I believe she has found the perfect man and that I am happy for her. She doesn't know that a man gives things like that in order to get something from you.

"What do you do for him?" I ask.

She looks confused. "What do you mean?"

"He has done all these really nice things. What does he want from you?"

She doesn't answer my question. Instead, she laughs, rolls her eyes and says, "I'm going to the ladies room."

It was a fair question, I think. I cook and clean the house and wash Cameron's clothes, including his dirty, stained underwear. We have sex whenever he wants it. But, perhaps there is something more I should be doing. Perhaps Lyla knows something I don't. I observe Eric watching her, admiring her, as she moves across the room and feel a little jealous.

The wait staff brings French onion soup to the table.

The smell makes me feel nauseous. As I get up to follow Lyla to the bathroom, I glance toward the bar where Cameron is still sitting. He does not notice me. He does not watch me. I slip through the door into the hallway unnoticed.

# Chapter Eight

"I like Lyla," I tell Cameron on the way home from the party. "She's really nice."

He grunts in response. He is very drunk and slouched in the passenger seat of our car. Neither of us say anything else. He is asleep by the time we arrive at our house.

"Cameron. Cameron." I touch his shoulder, then shake him lightly. He has to wake up. I cannot carry him into the house. "Cameron!" I speak a little louder. He snores. I walk around the car and open his door. The cold air rouses him a little. "Cameron, you have to wake up. We're home."

He stumbles out of the car and up the steps. I grab my purse, lock the car, and follow him. He waits unsteadily by the front door until I punch in the security code and open it. He makes it to the couch before he collapses and is snoring again before I even hang up my coat. I cover him with a blanket and put a glass of water and two aspirin on the coffee table for him before heading up to bed.

Cameron is still sleeping when it is time for me to leave in the morning. I'm meeting Janey to go Christmas shopping. He has tossed the blanket on the floor during the night, so I pull it back over him and give him a kiss on the forehead. The aspirin is gone and the glass is empty so I know he got up at least once during the night.

"I'll be back soon," I whisper. He looks so peaceful, so sweet. Just in case he doesn't remember, I write a quick note about where I will be and leave it on the kitchen counter. I draw a heart next to my name, then add another smaller one next to it. I will tell him tonight about the baby.

I wrap myself in my warmest coat and put on a hat and thick gloves. I walk the six blocks to the bus stop and take the 9:45 a.m. bus to the mall just in case Cameron needs the car when he wakes up.

"You're awfully quiet," Janey says to me as we sit down for coffee in the food court. "What's going on?"

I hesitate, then tell her, "I'm pregnant."

She looks at me with curiosity. "Are you happy about that?"

"Yes," I say hesitantly. "But please don't say anything. It's a bit embarrassing, you know, that, well, that it happened."

Janey laughs. "You're married, Amelia. It's perfectly fine to have sex and to have babies. People would think you were odd if you didn't. What did Cameron say about the two of you having a baby?"

"I haven't told him yet."

She looks at me, eyes squinting. "Why not?"

I hug myself and rock back and forth a couple of times. "I'm telling him tonight. I—I want it to be special. We didn't plan on a baby so soon, but I think he'll be thrilled about it."

"And if he's not?"

"He will be." My voice sounds a bit shaky. I repeat myself, trying to sound more confident. "I think he would have liked it to be his decision, but he will be happy about it anyway," I tell Janey. I know he will either be happy about his ability to get me pregnant or mad at me for failing to follow his orders to use birth control. I'll have to admit to him that I forgot to bring my birth control pills to Vermont.

"Uh huh." Janey does not sound convinced. "Well, I'm happy for you. How are you feeling?

"A bit nauseous in the mornings, but not too bad."

"That's good."

We finish our coffee and stand up. Janey gives me a hug. "I'm here for you, sweetie. Don't hesitate to let me know if you need anything, understand?"

I nod. I'm feeling better now. Janey does that. She has a way of making everything seem just fine.

We finish our shopping a few hours later and Janey gives me a ride home. She helps me carry the packages into the house. I am relieved to see that Cameron is no longer asleep on the couch. I hear him rattling dishes in the kitchen.

"Cameron, I'm home!" I call to him.

"Where were you?" he asks accusingly, coming into the living room.

"At the mall—Christmas shopping with Janey. I left you a note."

"No you didn't." The scowl leaves his face when he sees Janey standing next to me.

"Oh, hello," he says to her. "You must be Janey. Nice to meet you." Cameron shakes her hand.

"Nice to finally meet you, too," Janey says politely.

There is an awkward silence before Cameron says, "Thanks for bringing Amelia home." He walks to the front door and holds it open.

"You're welcome," Janey says. She looks at me, one eyebrow raised.

"Yes, thank you!" I say. "I'll see you tomorrow at work."

She nods.

Cameron closes the door behind her, and his scowl returns. "Why didn't you tell me where you were? I was worried!"

"I left you a note on the counter." I clearly remember leaving a note for him.

"No, Amelia, you didn't. There is no note."

I walk to the kitchen to show him where I left it. He's right. There is no note. Why is there no note? I look on the floor and under the dishes on the table. There is no note. "I'm sorry, Cameron. I was sure I left it here for you."

"Well, no matter, you're home safe. That's all that matters." He pulls me close and kisses my hair. "Just don't do that again, alright?"

"Alright," I say, squeezing my eyes shut, trying very, very hard to remember if I wrote the note. I'm not sure now. "Let me start dinner. I want to do something special for you."

I walk to the sink to wash my hands. "Oh," I say, startled. "I'm sorry I left the sink so dirty." I run a finger through the film covering the bottom. It feels a bit like ashes.

"No problem," Cameron says, turning on the water. He rinses the sink. "There, you see? It's clean again." He smiles and lifts my chin with a finger so I am looking into his warm, brown eyes. He leans down to give me a kiss and I forget what I was going to ask him. "Now, what's for dinner?" he asks.

"What would you like?"

"Steak, I think."

"Okay." There are steaks in the freezer so I won't have to run to the grocery store.

"Oh, and make those cheesy mashed potatoes like my mom does."

"Okay," I say, hoping I have remembered to buy cheese. I open the refrigerator to check. I relax and breathe again when I see a block of Velveeta on the bottom shelf. I quickly thaw the steak in the microwave and put it on the grill, setting a timer so it cooks to medium rare—exactly the way Cameron likes it. I have just enough time to boil the potatoes and put the asparagus in the oven to roast. I pour a drink of water for both of us, set the table, and light a candle, hoping for a romantic evening. I have important news to share.

I wait until Cameron is full and about to push his chair back before I speak.

"Wait." I cover his hand with mine. He looks at me, surprised. I have never given him a command. It seems a bit awkward, even for me. Cameron raises an eyebrow and looks at me quizzically. "I need to tell you something," I say, letting go of his hand.

"What?" He seems impatient. It's 6:00 p.m. and the news is on.

I hesitate for a moment, not sure how he will react. "I'm pregnant." When he doesn't answer, I add, "We're going to have a baby."

I wait for his smile, his exclamation of joy, but there is nothing. He still doesn't speak. I twist my napkin under the table nervously.

"Okay," he finally says. "When?"

"I think August. I haven't gone to the doctor yet."

"Oh, so you could be mistaken."

"No. No, I'm sure," I say, meeting his eyes. "I haven't had a period in almost two months so I did the home pregnancy test. It was positive."

"Hmmm," he says. "You have some paid leave available, right? You'll have to keep working after that runs out. You know that, right? We need the money."

"Oh." I had assumed Cameron would want me to stay home. "I thought I would stop working at the accounting office and take care of her—or him. Who will watch the baby, if not me?"

"My mother will watch the baby, of course."

My heart sinks. "What about working part-time? Could I do that? I don't want to be a burden on your mother."

"Absolutely not."

"But if your mother says she can't do it and we have to hire a babysitter or send the baby to daycare, that will cost more than I make. It doesn't make sense." I am trying not to cry. He can't see me cry. That will just make him angry.

"You should have thought of that before you got pregnant." He leans back and crosses his arms. I know he wants to hit me. I see his hands twitching underneath his elbows.

He's right again, of course. I am the one responsible for birth control and I failed. We agreed when we got married not to have children for at least five years and I have broken that agreement. I pick up the dishes and carry them to the sink, trying desperately to hold back the tears. I retreat into my head. It's the only way to stop the tears from spilling over. *Stupid, stupid, stupid*, I scold myself. I think about work. I think about the chores I have to do tonight. And then I think about singing. That makes me smile, and I forget for a brief moment that I have created such a huge problem.

I hear Cameron get up and go into the living room. He turns on the TV. I hear the newscaster's voice but can't make out any of his words. I stand still with my hands in the dishwater and close my eyes. The phone rings.

"Hey, Mom," I hear Cameron say. "I'm glad you called. I have a favor to ask. Amelia just told me she's pregnant, so—"

A squeal of delight interrupts him. Lorna sounds happy about this. I walk into the room, and Cameron puts the phone on speaker so I can hear, too.

"Oh, darling, that's wonderful! I'm so excited for you."

"Congratulations, Cameron," Laurence says, joining the conversation. "You're a real man now. Always knew you had it in you."

"Thanks, Dad." Cameron finally smiles at me. "Did it without even trying. Piece of cake."

Laurence and Lorna laugh. They don't ask how I'm feeling. It's okay. I let them have their moment with Cameron.

"Anyway, Mom. I was hoping you would be available to watch the baby after it's born. Amelia has to go back to work, of course."

There is a moment of silence before Lorna says, "We'll cross that bridge when we come to it. Don't worry. Just enjoy this time, this experience. I've got to call everyone. Oh my! I'm going to be a grandmother!"

Cameron chuckles and says in a shaky, elderly voice. "Grandma and Grandpa. That's what we'll call you from now on."

"Don't you dare," Lorna says. I can hear the amusement and affection in her voice, though.

Cameron hangs up and grabs me around the waist. He swings me around and kisses me before letting go.

I sigh in relief as he smiles and puts a hand on my belly.

"I really did it? I put a baby in there?" he asks in wonder.

"Yes," I assure him. "You did it."

# Chapter Nine

It's now March and I'm beginning to show. I'm embarrassed, but Cameron thinks it's cute. He points out the little bulge to all of his friends. "See, I knocked her up. Pretty quick, too." He likes to boast about it. I think it's getting on their nerves a bit. They laugh, but quickly change the topic of conversation to something else. Eric and Lyla are getting married in June so Lyla likes to talk about that.

Eric and Lyla arrive at my house early on Saturday morning. He and Cameron are going to the gun range, and they thought I would like the company. I don't mind. Lyla's nice, and she does most of the talking so I don't have to worry about what to say.

"I'd ask you to be a bridesmaid, Amelia," Lyla tells me after the men leave. "But you'll be huge by then. The dresses I've picked out are form-fitting and would look horrible on you. Oh! No offense! I hope to get pregnant just as quickly as you did. You are so lucky!" She seems a bit flustered and stares into the cup of coffee I have made for her.

"I really don't mind," I tell her sincerely. I much prefer to be in the background in any setting. "You're very considerate to think about things like that."

I feel a sharp twinge of pain near my navel. I ignore it. "Tell me about the dresses."

"Oh! They are a beautiful shade of lavender with a big bow that ties in the back—"

She tells me more, but I don't really hear any of it. I smile and nod and try not to clutch my belly. The pain gradually fades.

"I have got to go," Lyla tells me after a while. "Eric is taking me to hear a wedding band. We'd ask Cameron's band to play, but we want him to enjoy the wedding, not work it." She's frowning and looks at me with a bit of trepidation.

I smile at her. "I'm sure he would rather just be there, celebrating with you. Please don't worry about it."

"Good!" she says. "Okay, then. See you soon!"

Lyla lets herself out and I curl up on the couch. The pain is back. It squeezes my belly so hard I can hardly breathe, but it comes and goes so I try not to worry.

Cameron doesn't come back until after dinner. I've put his plate in the refrigerator for another day. "Sorry I'm so late, babe." He leans down and gives me a kiss on the top of my head. "My cousin Fred is in town, and you know how it is when we get together."

I do know how it is. The two of them tell jokes and make fun of people and gang up with each other to tease anyone else who might happen to be with them. It is funny to a point, but they take it too far. I am very glad I was not with him today.

"So how was your day?" I am touched that he asks. "Did you and Lyla have a good time?"

"Yes."

"Great." He goes to the refrigerator and gets a beer.

"Cameron?" I reach out for him.

"What?" He sits in the armchair and turns on the TV.

"I've had a little pain today."

"I'm sure that's normal, right? You start to feel weird things around the end of the second trimester? You're what, six months pregnant now?" He flips the channels and doesn't even look at me.

"It doesn't feel normal."

"Well, let me know if it gets worse."

"Okay," I say. "I'm going to get ready for bed."

"Sure." He's not listening.

I go into the bathroom and brush my teeth. I feel something wet trickling down my leg. It feels like I've peed my pants. I go into the bedroom to get a change of underwear and my pajamas. Before I go back into the bathroom, I grab a handheld mirror and take it with me. I can feel something in my vagina. I am scared, but I push the emotion to the back of my mind. No need to panic. I'm fine. I'm sure everything is fine.

I sit on the toilet and hold the mirror so I can see. There is a very tiny, perfectly formed foot about the size of my thumbnail protruding from my vagina. I stare at it. Five tiny toes. A heel. An arch. It looks like a doll's foot. It takes me a moment to realize that this is my baby's foot. I let out a wail. It startles Cameron and he comes running.

"What is it?"

"There's a—there's a—foot—coming out." I am sobbing.

He dials the doctor's number and hands me the phone. His face is as ashen as mine. He's frightened. I am crying too hard to speak, but Cameron won't help me. I manage to get out the words, "baby's foot—in my vagina."

The doctor understands and tells me to get to the hospital immediately. I am to lie down in the backseat of the car and Cameron is to drive me. Do I understand? I nod, even though he cannot see me. He repeats, "Do you understand?"

"Yes," I whisper. I hang up and tell Cameron what we have to do. He gets the keys and I follow him out to the car. I can't feel. I can't think. I just put one foot in front of the other until I am in the car with my eyes shut tightly so I can not see anything real, anything that is different from the way I want it to be.

It takes about thirty minutes to get to the emergency room. The doctor is waiting for me, and I am taken to a delivery room right away. I reach for Cameron as they wheel me away, but he has his back to me and is talking on his phone.

"Can Cameron—my husband—come?" I ask haltingly.

"Of course," the nurse says. "We'll let him know where you are."

"Thank you," I say, closing my eyes.

I don't say anything as the doctor examines me or when he tells me that it is too late—the baby is dead. The nurse sets up a Petocin drip in my IV. "To speed up the labor," she tells me. "I'm sorry you have to go through this, but it's the best way to get the fetus out."

"*Baby*," I say in my head. "*It is my <u>baby</u>.*"

Once the IV is running, they leave the room. It is so quiet in here. I lie still, counting the tiles on the ceiling. There is no pain now. The nurse must have put something in the IV. I feel nothing.

An hour goes by. I know it has been an hour because I am counting seconds and I have reached three thousand, six hundred. I wonder how much longer it will be until

Cameron comes to be with me. The door opens, but it is not Cameron. It's the nurse. She comes to check on me. She lifts the sheet between my legs and says, "Oh!" before running back out of the room. She is back in sixty-three seconds with the doctor.

"That was fast," he says. The nurse holds out a plastic container. I watch the doctor put my tiny baby in it.

"Is it a boy or a girl?" I ask.

He looks at me oddly. I can tell he does not want to answer. "A girl," he says, finally.

She is so small, so fragile, so perfect. If I could hold her, she would fit in the palm of my hand, her legs about half the length of my longest finger. I get just a glimpse of her before the nurse carries her out of the room in the plastic container that looks like Tupperware. I want to know what they will do with her, but I am afraid to ask.

"We're going to do a D and C now," the doctor tells me. "Just to be sure everything is removed."

I don't give permission. I don't say anything. I just close my eyes and wish that Cameron was here as I'm wheeled down the hall toward the operating room.

"Where were you?" I ask Cameron the next morning when he comes to pick me up at the hospital. "I needed you with me."

He shrugs as if it is nothing and says, "Fred came to the hospital. He was worried. I could hardly leave him sitting in the waiting room by himself, could I? He entertained me with stories and jokes and kept my mind off things. It was really nice of him, don't you think?"

*No,* I think, but I don't say. *No. What would have been nice is if you had been with me.*

We drive home in silence and never speak of it again.

# Chapter Ten

I'm back at work now. I used a week of vacation so I would not have to tell anyone at the office that I was in the hospital. Janey knows, though. She sees it in my face. We eat lunch in silence today. I can't speak, and she doesn't know what to say. I stare at the sandwich on the table in front of me. It seems like too much of an effort to pick it up, so I just let it sit there in the stuffy air. At one point, Janey reaches over and takes my hand, giving it a gentle, comforting squeeze. It's the best she can do. It's the best anyone can do. I am grateful and give her hand a squeeze back before standing up to take my lunch to the trash.

"We can talk about it when you're ready," she whispers to me as we head back to our desks. I nod, knowing I will never talk about it. It is too painful. I must move on. At least, that is what Cameron says. *Just move on. Stop being so morose. We can have more.*

I bury the sadness. I don't think about it. I don't talk about it. I don't allow it to control me, and I discover the good thing about suppressing the sadness, about withdrawing into yourself—time passes unnoticed. The world moves on and sweeps you along with it.

It is May. Cameron brings me flowers. "Just because I love you," he tells me, giving me a kiss. I smell the flowers and put them in a vase on the kitchen table. I forget to add water and they wilt within a day. Thankfully, Cameron does not notice.

Then, it is June. Lyla and Eric get married. I am there. She is beautiful in her ivory lace gown. They look at each other with so much love as they say their vows and I try to be happy for them. I try to feel anything.

August arrives quietly. Cameron's family takes us to Florida. I stand in the ocean, feeling the waves push against me. I don't resist and let them take me down. It is quiet and peaceful underneath the water. Cameron pulls me up. "Geez, Amelia. You've got to be careful!" he scolds me as he takes me to the blanket on the beach and tells me to stay there.

For some reason, people like October. Janey puts Halloween decorations on my desk. She has chosen black cats and pumpkins that stare blankly at me, a mirror image of my own visage.

November brings the cold weather. Lorna tells me how to cook a turkey properly. I try to ignore her, but she watches over my shoulder. *"More salt, Amelia. You should use celery in the stuffing, Amelia. There are not enough bread crumbs, Amelia. Oh, that will come out so dry, Amelia. Lower the oven temperature, Amelia."* After a while, I just do what she says. It is easier that way.

How did December come so quickly? I decorate the artificial tree Cameron put in front of the living room window. He sits in his armchair, watching. His body language tells me whether I am putting the ornaments in the correct places. He gets up only once to adjust the one with his favorite football team logo. I feel I have done well, but it doesn't really matter. They will all come down in a few weeks.

I am on autopilot. I go and do and act the way I am supposed to, but without thought, without emotion.

It is the end of March now and I remember our baby's birthday. And her death day. One year ago today. I leave work early and walk about a mile until I find myself standing in front of a stone church with heavy, elaborately carved wooden doors and a tall, round tower. It has somehow beckoned me. "Come," it whispers. "Come and find peace." The snow has melted, and I see crocuses blooming near the open wrought iron gate along the edge of the property.

"St. Philips Church Cemetery," I read the sign near the entrance. Most of the grave markers in the cemetery are at least one hundred years old. I wander through the well-kept yard and pause at each one, studying the names and dates. These were people who were loved and cared for, people who someone wanted to remember long after they were gone.

No one will remember my daughter. I was not able to bury her. They called her a fetus and threw her away like she was just medical waste. I stop in front of a small grave marker with an angel on the top of it. "Abigail May Huxley, born Mar 27, 1876, died Mar 27, 1876," I read. The significance stuns me and I drop to my knees. A tear rolls down my cheek.

Abigail May Huxley's life had been as short as my daughter's. She lived hardly at all. I know nothing more than that about this child, but I feel a connection to her. I run my fingers lovingly across the engraving on the marker.

I didn't name my daughter last year, but I do now. She is Abigail May. I close my eyes and imagine that this is my daughter's grave. I can come here anytime I wish to visit her, to remember her. She even has an angel watching over her.

My smile is real. It is the first time I have smiled in a year. I touch the angel on the headstone and whisper, "Thank you."

When I walk back to the office, where Cameron is coming to pick me up, I feel relief. The sadness that has followed me like a dark cloud is gone.

"Where were you?" Cameron asks angrily. He is sitting in the car, drumming irritably on the steering wheel. I glance at my watch. The hands read 5:05 p.m. I am five minutes late.

"Sorry," I tell him. "I went for a quick walk."

"It was rude to keep me waiting."

"Sorry," I repeat.

"Just don't do it again."

I turn my head away and look out the window. I *had* wanted to tell him about Abigail May, but now I don't. Keeping her all to myself makes me feel like I have a bit of power I didn't have before and I like it. I smile for the second time today.

# Chapter Eleven

Janey and I have resumed our talks at work. I am even allowed to see her on weekends occasionally, when Cameron has plans to see his own friends and doesn't mind if I don't come along.

"You seem happy again," Janey says as we walk around the mall on Saturday afternoon.

"I am." I smile and link my arm in hers.

She raises an eyebrow. "Spill it! I know there's something going on."

"There's nothing going on. I just—well, made peace, I guess, with losing the baby. I feel forgiven, like she's happy in Heaven with the angels and not angry with me any more for not taking better care of her." I don't tell Janey about the grave just yet. I hug the memory of it. Maybe I will take her there one day soon, though, so she can understand.

"You know the miscarriage wasn't your fault, Amelia." Janey looks incredulous. "You didn't do anything to cause it."

"You don't know that. Maybe I did something by accident because I didn't know any better."

"Okay, then. Tell me. What did you do?"

"Noth—I don't know—but it must have been something. Why else would…" I am trying not to cry.

Janey hugs me again. "Oh, honey. These things sometimes just happen for no reason. It was nothing you did or didn't do. Okay?"

I nod. "Let's get lunch," I say to change the subject. I don't want to talk about this anymore.

"Sure," Janey says. "Let's get lunch."

We walk past a small store with the most beautiful dress I have ever seen displayed in the window. I pause. It is an emerald green color with a sweetheart neckline, a form-fitting waist, and a full, flowing, knee-length skirt.

"Let's go in," Janey says, pulling me after her.

"No, I—"

"We should have some fun today! When was the last time you had a new dress?"

"Actually, I can't remember. My wedding dress, of course. But other than that, I don't know."

"Then, it's the perfect day to at least look." Janey smiles and pulls the green dress off a rack in the middle of the store and holds it up to me.

"This is beautiful! Try it on."

I take it and duck into a changing room.

"I want to see you in it!" Janey calls from outside the door. She knows me. I had no intention of putting it on. Now, I suppose I will have to.

The fabric is soft. I run my fingers over it. It really is beautiful, but not so fancy that I couldn't wear it to work. I look at the price tag. It says $118. Oh well, that's too expensive for me.

Janey knocks at the door. "Do you have it on?"

"No. It costs too much money."

"Put it on anyway. That's the fun part! Even if you don't buy it, it's still fun to try it on and model it a bit."

I laugh. "Okay." I step out of my clothes and slip it on over my head. Janey opens the door.

"I'm impatient," she says. "Oh my! You are stunning in that dress! It brings out the green in your eyes."

I look in the mirror. I'm not sure I agree about the stunning part, but my eyes are definitely green.

"I can't buy it, Janey. It's over a hundred dollars."

"Did you only bring a hundred dollars with you? Do you need to borrow some money? I would be happy to lend you the extra twenty dollars if you need it. And lunch is on me, so don't worry about that."

"No, it's not that. I have a credit card I can use, but Cameron and I promised each other we would never spend over a hundred dollars without consulting each other and agreeing on the purchase. It's part of our budgeting plan."

"Oh," Janey says, frowning. "Well, hopefully you'll ask him about this. That dress is perfect for you."

"I'll think about it," I tell her, knowing full well that I won't. It's not worth the fight. Cameron thinks I have enough clothes, and he hates when I spend any money.

We don't talk about it over lunch. Instead, Janey tells me about the trip she is planning to Mexico with her son and his family. She makes me laugh with her stories. Lunch is over too soon, and it's time to go.

I'm home before Cameron. That's always a good thing. He comes in the door, smiling.

"Did you have a good time with Eric?" I ask him, taking his coat and hanging it up in the hall closet.

"The best!" he says, grinning. "We came up with a new tune that is out-of-this-world good. I'm sure it will be a number one hit if we can get a radio station to play it."

"Wow!" I am happy for him. "Can you sing it for me?"

He looks at me sideways. "Are you kidding? It wouldn't sound the same without the whole band. Maybe you should have been there instead of out with Janey."

I have attended a few band rehearsals with him. He makes me sit in a corner and be quiet. They all just ignore me. I asked once if I could sing with them and they just laughed. I don't even know if Cameron remembers that I can sing. I don't think their singer is all that good, but what do I know?

"You don't really want me there."

"No, we don't."

I can't tell if he's kidding or not, but I smile as if I think he is.

"I'm going back to Eric's house later so we can finish the recording."

"I'll be here at home, waiting for you," I tell him.

He rolls his eyes and shakes his head, like I just made a bad joke. "What's for dinner?" he says.

"There's chicken and potatoes in the crockpot. I put it in this morning before I went out with Janey. I just have to make a vegetable to go with it."

"Can you hurry? I'm really hungry."

"Of course," I say, pulling the green beans out of the refrigerator. "It will take about fifteen minutes to roast these."

"Fine," Cameron says, heading off to the bathroom with a magazine. "Call me when it's ready."

He eats in record time. I know he's anxious to get back to his music, and I can't blame him for that. I know what it's like to have an idea and want to write it down or record it before it disappears. He gives me a quick kiss on the cheek as he goes out the door. "Don't wait up," he says. "I have no idea how long it will take us to get this right."

"Okay," I say. "See you later."

He's been gone only about an hour when my phone rings. The caller ID says it's Tyrese, a friend of Cameron's from college who we haven't seen in a few years and I would be happy to never, ever see him for the rest of my life. During my last year in college, Tyrese would try to touch me, just like the boys in high school. No, more than the boys in high school. I shiver with fear, remembering how he pushed me up against a wall and pulled up my skirt, his fingers going places they should not go, his mouth on my breasts. I had tried to call out for help, but students passing by just laughed and pointed. When he finally let me go, I ran back to my dorm room and vomited for hours.

When Cameron came to see me that night, I told him everything.

Cameron laughed. "Geez, Amelia. Tyrese was just joking, of course. You should loosen up and get over it." When I couldn't stop sobbing, he patted my back and said, "I'll talk to him, okay? I'll tell him to stop."

Cameron must have said something because Tyrese stopped following me. So, why is Tyrese calling me now? How did he get my number? I had hoped he had forgotten all about me.

"Hello?"

"Hello." He speaks with a deep, measured tone that scares me. "You know, you really should lock your doors when Cameron leaves the house." He chuckles. It sounds menacing.

I am upstairs. I hear the front door open and close. I hang up the phone and run into the bathroom, locking the door behind me. I hear Tyrese calling out, "Amelia? Where are you? Have you missed me? Let me feel those beautiful tits again. Come on, baby, I've come back home just for you." He sounds drunk. Or high. Or both. "You should never have rejected me in college, Amelia. You need to pay for that."

I dial Cameron. "What do you want?" He sounds bothered.

"Cameron, there's someone in the house. Tyrese—Tyrese called my phone and said I should have locked the doors, and now he's in the house. I'm afraid! Please come home. Please!"

"Amelia, I can't come home right now. We're rehearsing. I'm sure everything's fine. Just go make him coffee or something."

"No, Cameron, you don't understand. I think he's going to hurt me or something."

"That's insane, Amelia. You're acting crazy. I've gotta go." Cameron hangs up. He's not coming and I'm not sure what to do. If Cameron thinks I'm crazy, the police probably will, too.

I hear Tyrese's footsteps on the stairs. "Amelia?"

"I'm in the bathroom!" I call out. "I may be a while. Cameron will be home soon." I lie.

"Really?" He doesn't sound like he believes me.

"Yes. I've just called him. He's not too far away so he'll be back any minute now."

Tyrese doesn't answer. He just jiggles the door knob. I sit with my back against the door, my legs extended so that they are braced against the opposite wall.

"In fact, why don't you meet him at the bar on the corner instead of here? I'm sure he'll be happy to buy you a drink. The two of you can come back afterward. It will give me time to make a nice desert for you while you're gone. I'll just call him back and let him know that's what you're doing."

"I'll wait here," Tyrese says. I hear him unbuckling his belt.

"Oh, no. You can't do that," I tell him, trying to keep the panic out of my voice. "I will be quite a while in the bathroom, so I can't entertain you properly. And Cameron gets very jealous, you know. He has quite a temper, as I'm sure you remember from college. He will hurt you so badly—friend or not—if he thinks you were here alone with me for any length of time. Just go, have a drink with Cameron. It will be just like the old days, in college, you know."

I hear the floorboard outside the bathroom squeak as Tyrese shifts his weight. He's thinking about what I said. He has witnessed the damage Cameron's temper has done to other people. I am praying that the threat of that will be enough to stop him.

I hear the *click, click* of a switchblade opening and shutting, opening and shutting. The sound fades as he walks back down the stairs. The front door opens and shuts. Is it a trick? I get up and look out the window. I see Tyrese walking down the block, away from the house. Quickly, I run down the stairs and lock the front door. I check the back door, the garage door, and all of the windows in the house to make sure he can't get back in. Then, I take a pillow, a blanket, and my phone, and go back upstairs, locking myself in the bathroom. I am not coming out until Cameron gets home. I can't stop the shaking, but I don't cry. Instead, I retreat into my own mind, where it is safe and nothing bad ever happens to me.

It is midnight when Cameron finally comes home. I wake up to him pounding on the bathroom door.

"I've got to pee!" he says angrily. "Hurry up in there."

I unlock the door and come out, wrapped in the blanket and holding the pillow.

"What the heck?" he says. "Were you sleeping in there?"

"I was afraid of Tyrese, so I locked myself in the bathroom."

"You've been in there the whole time? Geez, you really act crazy sometimes." Cameron moves around me and stands in front of the toilet. "Go to bed, Amelia. Geez," he says again, shaking his head.

I obey. Of course, I obey. I always do whatever Cameron wants. I feel a bit of resentment push its way up in my consciousness, but I quickly shove it back down. "A good wife never complains," I remember my mother telling me when my father was late for dinner, or didn't show up at all, or brought home female clients, or drank too much, or hit her. She never spoke a harsh word about anyone. I'm sure my father had something to do with her falling down the stairs when I was fourteen, but when the paramedics asked what happened, she told them she was clumsy and just fell. She was one hundred percent loyal to her family. I need to be more like her.

"I'm sorry I interrupted your rehearsal," I tell Cameron as he climbs into bed.

He grunts and turns on his side, facing away from me. "Turn off the light, will you?" he mumbles.

I get out of bed, turn off the light, and stand in the dark for a moment, listening to Cameron breathe. He sounds peaceful, relaxed. I crawl back into bed and snuggle up to him. The faint, but pleasant smell of a perfume that's not mine taunts me as I drift off to sleep.

# Chapter Twelve

"I'm pregnant," I tell Janey once I am sure no one else in the courtyard can hear us. I have been bursting to tell Janey the news all morning. We've chosen a picnic table at the far end of the courtyard for privacy. "I'm going to have a baby! The doctor says everything is fine. I have to be careful—no strenuous activities. I just know this one will be perfect."

"I'm so excited for you!" Janey gives me a hug. "How does Cameron feel about it?"

"Oh, he's thrilled. Cautious, but thrilled."

"Cautious?"

"Yes, well, he told me to be sure to do it right this time. You know, take care of myself, follow the doctor's instructions, and eat well."

"Does he think you didn't take care of yourself the last time?"

"Well, obviously, I didn't."

Janey holds my face between her hands and looks me straight in the eyes. "How many times do I have to tell you, it was not your fault?"

I push her hands away. What does she know, anyway? She's not a doctor. She is my friend, though—one I want to keep—so I *can't* be angry with her. I struggle to control my temper. "Okay," I say. "I believe you." I want to believe her, so it's only a half lie.

I take a bite of my sandwich. This pregnancy feels different. I'm not sick, like last time. I can actually eat. Food doesn't really taste good, but I have to eat. I'm feeding the baby now, not just myself.

"When is the baby due?" Janey asks me.

"In about five months—the middle of December."

"Oh! A Christmas baby! I love it. What a nice gift for you!"

I smile. "I know! I waited to say anything until I was sure everything was going well." A sudden pain in my belly makes me wince. It feels like my middle is being squeezed by a bear and I put both hands on my abdomen in alarm. It's a pain I remember too well.

"What is it?" Janey asks with concern.

I can't speak. I just look at her with wide, panicked eyes. A tear rolls down my cheek.

Janey picks up her phone and dials 9-1-1. "No," she says firmly. "This will not happen again."

The pain is gone by the time the paramedics arrive. I feel silly. "It's all in my head—just fear," I protest. Janey tells me I am going to the hospital anyway to be checked out, and then informs our boss that she is going with me to the hospital and he will have to give our work to someone else today. He nods and stays out of her way. Everyone stays out of Janey's way when she is in this mood. She takes charge, telling the paramedics all about my medical history and my current symptoms, and insists she will be riding in the back of the ambulance with me. They let her.

At the hospital, the doctor refers to Janey as my mother, and I don't correct him. She demands a variety of medical tests I have never heard of, and the doctor agrees. They have their heads together when the test results come back, whispering so I can't hear what they are saying.

"Amelia," Janey says, taking my hand after consulting with the doctor. "Your body went into labor, but the labor has stopped and the baby is fine. You are fine."

"That's the good news," the doctor says. "But, with your history, I would like to put you on complete bed rest and daily monitoring for the remainder of the pregnancy. If we need to give you medication to stop labor, we'll do that too. You are sixteen weeks pregnant now. I'd like to get you to at least thirty-two weeks if we can."

"The baby is fine?" I can only focus on one thing at a time.

"Yes. Did you hear what I said about *complete* bed rest?" The doctor looks at me sternly.

"Did anyone call Cameron?" I ask.

"Not yet," Janey says. "The doctor will call him and explain everything. In the meantime, I'm taking you home and putting you in bed."

"No. No, I can't. I have to work. I have to take care of Cameron."

"You *have* to be on bed rest twenty-four hours a day, every day, for at least sixteen more weeks." The doctor is annoyed, like I have been wasting his time. "If you want this baby, you need to do what I tell you."

"Okay." I look at Janey for reassurance. "Okay. I will."

The doctor leaves and Janey helps me get dressed. It takes fifty-four minutes before a nurse finally brings a wheelchair and the discharge paperwork.

Cameron appears in the doorway, out of breath and scowling.

"Why didn't you call me? They said I had to come immediately like it was an emergency or something. This doesn't look like an emergency."

"We were a little busy, Cameron," Janey says. "I asked the doctor to call you and it appears that he did since you are here. Late, of course. You missed the emergency part."

Cameron ignores Janey. "You should have called me, Amelia."

"I thought it was better to have the doctor call you," Janey continues. "He can explain things much better than we women can, of course. Man to man." I hear the sarcasm in her voice, but Cameron nods as if what she is saying is perfectly rational.

"The doctor said you went into labor, but you're fine now, so I'm here to take you home, Amelia."

"I'm coming with you," Janey says.

"There's no need."

"There is, actually, since I don't have a car here. I rode in the ambulance with her. The least you can do is give me a ride. Your house is closer to work than the hospital is, so I can get someone to pick me up from there."

"Fine." He turns around. "Come on, then."

Janey takes my arm and helps me into the wheelchair, sighing. She pushes it out the door and onto the elevator. "Why don't you go ahead and pull the car up to the front of the hospital?" she says to Cameron. "I'll stay with Amelia."

He exits the elevator at the ground floor without a word and hurries on ahead of us.

Janey gently squeezes my shoulder, to comfort me, I think. It does. I lean back in the wheelchair and close my eyes. I'm not worried about anything. Janey is here.

I don't remember getting in the car, or the ride home, or who pulled out the couch and made it into a bed so that I could see out the front window, or read a book, or watch TV for the next sixteen weeks. Whoever it was had also made sure my phone was plugged in and within reach. The first thing I remember is waking up the morning after my hospital visit on the couch with Cameron standing over me.

"What's for breakfast?" he asks. Does he really expect me to get up and make breakfast?

"I thought you would get an egg sandwich on your way to work?" My voice sounds timid and weak. "The doctor says I can only get up to use the bathroom."

Cameron rolls his eyes. "What am I supposed to do? Get all my meals out? We can't afford that if you're not working. Geez. I wish I had known you were defective before I married you."

Am I *defective*? It's a new thought. I guess I am. I am not able to have a normal pregnancy like everyone else. "I'm sorry, Cameron. Maybe your mother can help? Or I can call Janey or Lyla."

"You do that," he says, going out the front door and slamming it behind him.

But I don't have to call anyone. Janey shows up mid-morning with a laptop and a stack of files.

"The boss said you could work from home as long as the doctor cleared it. I know how important the income is for you. So, I spoke to your doctor this morning, and he said it would be fine as long as you could work in a reclined position. He doesn't want any pressure on the cervix."

"Janey, I'm so grateful! That was worrying me a bit."

"You don't need any additional stress. You need to be thinking only about yourself and that baby. I just brought you one project. We'll see how it goes. Did you eat this morning?"

"No. I didn't want to get up and Cameron had to get to work—"

"That idiot." Janey is not holding anything back. "You need to eat. You need protein." She goes into the kitchen, and it isn't long before I smell bacon and eggs cooking. My stomach growls. She props me up with a pillow behind my back before bringing me a cup of chamomile tea and a plate of scrambled eggs and bacon, which I devour within minutes.

"Thank you!" I can't remember the last time anyone did this for me. It's overwhelming.

"I will be back every day to pick up your work and make sure you are eating."

She takes the dirty dishes to the kitchen and comes back with a peanut butter and jelly sandwich wrapped in foil and a large jug of ice water with a straw. "This is for your lunch so you don't have to get up at all. Now, what's your mother-in-law's phone number?"

Janey calls Lorna and suggests that she provide some dinners for Cameron and me.

"Poor Cameron! Four months of this! I will, of course, be happy to take a turn providing dinners, and I'm sure Lyla will also help," I hear Lorna say. "I'll call her."

Lorna must have followed through on her promise because Lyla came in the door with Cameron and Eric at 5:00 p.m. carrying a bag of Chinese takeout. "There's plenty here for us tonight, and I'm sure there will be left-overs for you to heat up for at least one more day." Lyla seems proud that she has thought of it. The smell makes me a little nauseous, but I ignore it.

"Thank you, Lyla. You are so thoughtful!" I try to sound

cheerful. The three of them go into the kitchen and bring their plates back into the living room to eat with me. Cameron hands me a plate of chicken with broccoli. He knows it's my favorite. I'm touched. I smile up at him. "Thank you," I say. "This is perfect."

He leans down to give me a kiss. "Of course."

"Aww! Isn't that sweet?" Lyla teases. "The two love birds. I'm a bit jealous."

"Why would you be jealous?" The question pops out of my mouth before I can stop it. "I mean, you have a wonderful life."

"I guess," she says. Lyla and Eric exchange glances. "We've been trying to get pregnant, and so far nothing has happened."

That surprises me. I want to ask if she is defective, too, like me, but that seems a bit too personal. We eat in silence for a few minutes, but I can see Lyla and Eric are almost bursting with news they want to share.

"We saw a specialist last week." Eric sounds hopeful. "He says nothing is wrong. We're just trying too hard."

Lyla giggles and takes another bite of her food.

"I mean, we're just too stressed about the whole thing." Eric grins. "The doctor says to go out and buy a car or something so we have something else to think about for a while."

"Did you?" I ask. "Buy a car, I mean."

Lyla and Eric look at each other and burst out laughing. Cameron joins in the hilarity. The three of them can't stop. It is contagious, and I smile and chuckle, even though I'm not sure what we're laughing about.

"We—we—we bought—" Lyla is struggling to get the words out. She is out of breath from laughing. "A house!" they both say together.

"A house? That's wonderful!" I am happy for them.

"Yep," Lyla says. "If buying a car *might* help, then buying a house *certainly* will." She starts to laugh again.

"That's right," Eric says, still grinning. "We might even have twins, we're so far in debt!"

"Oh." I don't know what else to say.

Lyla suddenly looks guilty. "Amelia, you look tired. I'm so sorry! I think we're all finished with dinner. Let me wash the dishes and then we'll get out of your hair."

"I want to hear about the house," I tell her.

"Next time, darling. You need to rest." She disappears into the kitchen. Cameron and Eric go outside to wait for her. I get up to use the bathroom and brush my teeth. They are gone by the time I get back to the couch. I snuggle under the blanket and wait for Cameron to come in. I try to stay awake, but I can't. I'm exhausted. It's been a long day. I have a feeling it will be a very long sixteen weeks.

# Chapter Thirteen

I feel a little like a beached whale. I've heard people use that expression, but never fully understood what they meant until now. My stomach has grown to the size of a basketball and I am still not allowed to get up except to go to the bathroom or move from the couch to my bed. I've only cheated just a little, getting up occasionally to make easy dinners for us when I'm really bored. So far, so good.

It's been twelve weeks since my medical incarceration. I've watched the entire summer go by through the window, and can't remember how the outside air feels or what flowers smell like. The leaves will turn color soon, and I will miss that, too—except for what I can see through the dusty window panes in front of me. The baby kicks, and now I have to pee again.

It's Saturday and Cameron has gone out. He's been out a lot. I wish he would stay with me, but I understand. I'm boring. Nothing happens for me to talk about. I would love to hear about his work and what he does all day, but he's too busy to sit and chat. He has my work to do as well as his own. He mows the lawn, washes dishes, and runs the vacuum almost every day, so he deserves some "me" time of his own.

I hear the car pull into the garage. It's only mid-afternoon and Cameron is back. I am pleasantly surprised and quickly run a brush through my hair. He comes in with several large boxes.

"I bought a DVD player and a surround sound system," he tells me, unpacking the boxes. I can tell he is excited. He busies himself hooking it all up to our TV.

"How much did all of that cost?" I ask him.

"About five hundred dollars," he tells me without hesitation or guilt.

I cannot keep the anger from spilling out. It shows in my tone even as I say softly through gritted teeth, "I thought we agreed we wouldn't spend over a hundred dollars without consulting each other. We can't afford that right now."

"I deserve this, Amelia." Cameron's voice has risen several decibels. "I've had to do everything for you these past couple of months. I don't know why you would resent that I do something for myself as well."

I burst into tears. I can't help it. At that moment, the front door bursts open, and Janey comes in with gifts in her hands, followed by Lyla, Lorna, and a bunch of people from work. They all have gifts. "Surprise!" they shout.

I get up and waddle to the bathroom, shutting the door behind me. I hear Janey ask Cameron, "What is wrong?"

"Nothing," he says. "Why would you think something is wrong?"

I dry my eyes and splash water on my face before flushing the toilet. I want them to think I just had to pee.

Nothing can be wrong. I look in the mirror. My eyes are red, but I can say that's because I'm tired.

When I return to the living room, Cameron has removed the empty boxes and is talking to a young woman I don't know. They laugh together over what I think must be some shared joke. I hope they are not talking about me. The other ladies are seated around the room, chatting with each other. They hardly notice me. They have piled the gifts on the floor in front of the couch and hung streamers and blue balloons across the doorway to the dining room. I smell food.

"Mmm! Meatballs?" I ask as I lower my bulky figure back onto the couch.

"And cake." Lyla sits next to me and smiles as if she has a secret.

"Lyla?" I ask. "Did it work? Did buying the house work?"

"Now, Amelia. This day is about you. We wanted to give you a surprise baby shower. My news can wait," she says loudly enough for everyone to hear.

"Congratulations!" I am really happy for her. I hate the attention being on me and am relieved when the other ladies gather around Lyla and demand details. I shrink back into the cushions and close my eyes. I feel as if I am listening to a conversation underwater as I retreat into my own world, the world in my mind.

I am a little girl again, sitting on the bottom of the community pool, listening to the muffled laughter of other children as they play above me. They sound so far away, as if in a dream. It is peaceful at the bottom of the pool. I sit cross-legged and hold on to the weights I have brought with me until my lungs are bursting. Reluctantly, I let go and kick back to the surface. The other swimmers are getting out of the pool. It's time to go home, but I don't want to. I take a deep breath and let myself sink back down to the bottom, grabbing the weights so I stay there. I can hold my breath for two minutes. Two minutes of peace. I wish I had gills, like a fish, so I could stay down here forever.

"Oh my god!" I hear a muffled voice say just before the splash comes. A hand reaches for me and pulls. I resist. I want to stay here. I tighten my grip around the weights. Another splash. Now, there are two people tugging at me, one on each side. I let go of the weights.

"I'm fine," I say as we break through the surface of the water. "I just wanted a few more minutes."

They pull me out of the pool. My father is standing there, scowling. "You are such a brat," he tells me. "You scared these poor ladies. Now, apologize."

"I'm sorry," I tell the two ladies standing there in soaking wet clothes, even though I am not sorry. Someone hands them a towel as my father grips my arm and leads me away. When we are next to his car and no one is watching, he slaps me across the face. "If you pull something like that again, I'll make sure you drown. I will push your face under the water long enough to make sure you get what you wish." He smiles. Later, he takes me to the backyard, where he has filled a large metal tub with water and does exactly what he threatened to do. My mother runs out of the house with a camera, screaming at him. "I am recording this. I swear I will give this to the police if you don't let her go."

"She has to be punished," he says, but he lets go. I don't want to give him the satisfaction of hearing me choke or cough. I run into the woods behind the house before I vomit into the bushes. When I hear him coming, I climb a tree near the edge of the woods where I can hide and rest—and watch. My father has gone back into the yard and I can see my parents arguing. My father drags my mother by her hair over to the tub and holds her face just above the water. He laughs as she struggles and then lets go. She is crying. "I would never give anything to the police, you know that," she tells him. "I was just trying to—-"

"I don't care." My father gets into his car and drives away. I can still hear him laughing.

But it is Cameron who is laughing. Not my father. I shake my head to clear it. *Come back, Amelia, come back,* I tell myself. I am not the little girl anymore. I am the grownup me—pregnant and stuck on this couch, watching real people in the real world.

"I don't think I know you," I say to the woman who has made Cameron laugh and with whom he has spent so much time tonight. She has dark, short hair and is wearing tight pants and a blouse that shows more cleavage than I would ever be comfortable showing. She's not pretty. In fact, I think she looks more like a man than a woman. It's the large breasts that give her away. Definitely a woman. An ugly woman. It's very kind of Cameron to be so attentive.

"Oh, I'm Kerri, one of Cameron's co-workers. He invited me to the shower. I hope you don't mind. I did bring a gift!" She leans down to hug me.

"You didn't have to do that. And, of course, you are more than welcome," I tell her. The words do not match the tone of my voice. I do not want her here, laughing with my husband, feeding him cake, while I am confined to this couch. The smell of her perfume is vaguely familiar.

"Yes, well, okay, thanks." She stumbles over her words. Cameron takes her arm.

"Let me show you the house," he says. I see him wink at her. He is trying to cover for my rudeness by being super friendly. I will have to apologize later.

# Chapter Fourteen

I lie in bed, staring at the ceiling as the sun comes up. Today, I've reached thirty-six weeks and the doctor says that whatever happens now, the baby will be fine. I can get up. I can go outside. I can cook. I can do anything I want to! It scares me. I've been confined for so long, freedom seems unnatural.

I struggle to take a breath and shift my position to make it a little easier. I smell gas. I'm confused. Why would my house smell like gas?

"Cameron?" I reach over to shake him awake, but he is gone. I throw off the covers and get up. He's not in the bathroom. He's not in the living room. His car is not in the garage. As I move toward the kitchen, the smell gets stronger. I see a candle on the table that is burning with a large, blue flame. I blow it out and notice that the oven dial is on "broil," but the pilot light is out. The smell of gas is so strong, it chokes me. I open the kitchen window. It helps a little, but the smell is still overpowering. I stumble to the living room and open those windows, as well.

I pick up my phone and dial Cameron's number.

"What is it?" He's obviously annoyed.

"You're not here."

"You called me to tell me I'm not home? That's insane, Amelia. I don't have time for this."

"No. No. I called you to tell you something must be wrong with the stove. There's a strong smell of gas in the house."

"Did you leave the oven on last night?"

"No. I'm sure I shut it off. But it was on this morning. And the pilot light was out. Did you notice anything before you left this morning?"

"Of course not."

"Did you light a candle before you left?"

"Amelia, what are you babbling about?"

"It just seems strange that the gas was on and there was an open flame near the oven."

"You're telling me you turned on the oven and left a lit candle close to it? Oh my god, Amelia! You could have killed yourself. There could have been an explosion! Open the windows and, for goodness sake, blow out the candle!"

"I did those things. Should I call the fire department?"

"And have them ask you why you turned on the oven, blew out the pilot light, and lit a candle? They'll think you're crazy, Amelia. Maybe even suicidal. Just turn off the oven and open the windows."

"I don't think I turned *on* the oven, Cameron. And I don't remember lighting a candle."

"Of course, you did. Who else is there? Sometimes I worry about your mental health, Amelia. You've got to pull yourself together. How are you going to be a good mother if you can't even take care of yourself?"

I don't answer. Did I forget to turn the oven off last night? Pilot lights can go out on their own if there is a breeze or something, I'm sure. But I'm almost positive I did not light a candle. I'm afraid of fire.

"It sounds like you have everything under control, then. I've got to go. My class starts in three minutes."

"Okay," I say. "Sorry I bothered you."

"Amelia, it's not a bother. It's just that you do such odd things. This one was very dangerous. You worry me. Don't do it again."

"I won't," I say.

Cameron hangs up.

Janey is coming to pick me up around eleven today. I feel a little rebellious since I haven't told Cameron about going out today, but he doesn't like Janey and would have told me not to go. I double-check the oven to make sure it is off before going to take my shower and get ready.

"I'm taking you out to lunch to celebrate your release," Janey says when she arrives. "Just you and me."

"Thanks!" I say, giving her a hug. It feels odd to be standing.

"Let me know if you get tired or feel anything happening in there." She waves a hand toward my huge belly.

"I will."

"We'll take it easy, anyway." She opens the door for me and takes my arm.

"I'm not an invalid anymore," I tell her, smiling. "I'm fine."

"I know," she says. "I'm just being a mother hen, watching out for my friend."

"You're sweet."

We don't talk much on the way to the restaurant. I am content to watch the landscape pass by. The trees are bare, with crooked branches reaching up as if to catch the last of the warm, late autumn sun. I roll down the car window and take a deep breath. "It's good to feel the wind on my face! It smells a little like it might snow. Thanksgiving is only a week away, you know. It always snows around Thanksgiving."

Janey smiles and pulls into the restaurant's parking lot. "It's too cold to get a table outside today, but I can ask for a table near the window if you like, so you can enjoy the view."

"Janey?" I hesitate. "Can we skip lunch and just go sit in the park for a while?"

"Sure," she says, turning the car around. "No problem."

"Wait. There's something I want to show you. Do you know where St. Philips Church is?"

"The one near our office?"

"Yes."

"I know where it is. Why?"

"Can we go there? I want to show you something. It's a secret. I've never told anyone else about it."

Janey puts on the blinker and we turn left and head toward St. Philips Church. I love that she never questions me or thinks I'm crazy. She accepts me for who I am.

"Here, turn in here." I point to the cemetery entrance. Janey raises an eyebrow but steers the car toward the open gate. She pulls off to one side of the small dirt road and shuts off the car.

"Why are we here?"

"Just come with me." I get out and she follows me to the small headstone with the angel. I stand in front of it, not speaking. She notices the dates right away.

"Oh, Amelia." She is crying softly.

I reach over and take Janey's hand. "I imagine this is my daughter. Abigail May Dallas." I trace the name on the headstone with my finger. "I never want to forget that she existed."

Janey puts her arm around my waist and gives me a hug. "This is so special, Amelia. Thank you for sharing it with me. I will come here, too, and bring flowers, to honor your daughter."

"Thanks, Janey." I turn my attention to the stone under the angel. "Abigail May, this is your little brother," I say, putting a hand on my swollen belly. I imagine them playing together, having little arguments like siblings do, and then laughing and skipping, arm in arm, down the road to school each day.

We stand in silence for a few more minutes, then I take Janey's hand and lead her away. I am glad I introduced her to Abigail May. Glad someone else knows and will remember my daughter besides me. But, I'm tired now and want to go home. That's enough for today.

"It's been a lovely day. Thank you, Janey," I say as she drops me off at my house thirty minutes later.

"My pleasure, honey." Janey pats my hand as I reach for the door handle. "I know you must have been anxious to get out of the house after all this time on the couch. Call me if you need anything. I'll check in with you tomorrow, okay?"

"Okay."

Cameron opens the front door for me. "Where have you been?"

"Janey thought I could use some time out of the house."

"You didn't leave me a note or send me a text," he says accusingly. "I was worried. Especially after what you did this morning."

"I—" I am about to tell him that I did leave a note, but realize he's right this time. "I didn't. I'm sorry. You're never home this early. I thought I would be back before you."

"Still, it would have been nice to know what you were doing and where you were."

"Uh huh," I mumble. I do not want him to know where I've been or what I've done.

"What was that?" Cameron's temper is rising. I can almost feel it heating up the air around us. His right hand balls into a fist, and he hits me on the jaw. I am surprised. Usually, he strikes or kicks where the bruises will not show, but I am pregnant, and he doesn't dare hit me in the stomach.

"I'm sorry, Cameron. It was thoughtless of me. You are right, of course. I will try to do better." The words fall out of my mouth. I don't even have to think about them anymore. It's automatic.

Cameron grunts. He's satisfied now that he has punished me and I have repented.

"I'm going to rest for a bit," I tell him.

He just grunts, grabs a beer, and sits on the couch. He turns on the television and I know I'm safe, for now. I crawl under the covers on my bed and try to sleep, but even the slightest noise makes me jump. The sound of Cameron shouting at the television terrifies me and I think he's coming for me again. He doesn't but I still cannot relax. My jaw aches. The baby kicks. When it is dark outside, I finally get up and walk slowly into the living room.

"Good, you're up," he says. "What's for dinner? The doctor said you can resume normal activities now, right? It's six o'clock and I'm starving."

I haven't thought about dinner. My stomach growls. "I'll throw something together really fast." I don't even know what's in the refrigerator. He does. Why doesn't *he* make something for me? I push that ill-tempered thought away quickly and hurry to the kitchen. That was selfish. What is wrong with me?

We eat and head off to bed early. I am worried that Cameron will think sex is included with resuming normal activities, but he doesn't seem interested. I am relieved. He rolls over right away and is sound asleep before I even finish brushing my teeth. I crawl into bed and close my eyes.

A pain in my belly wakes me around 5:00 am. I feel the muscles tighten and release. I ignore it. It happens again about ten minutes later, so I get up. By the time I finish my shower, the pains are coming every five minutes and getting stronger.

"Cameron?" I shake him. "Cameron? I think I'm in labor."

"What?" He rubs his eyes and sits up. "Now? It's early."

"The contractions are five minutes apart."

"Call the doctor," he tells me. "See what he says. You don't look like you're in a lot of pain to me."

The doctor tells me to come to the hospital right away. Cameron grumbles, but gets dressed. Janey has packed me a "to go" bag. I grab it and head for the car, stopping only to catch my breath when the pain hits.

Even though I feel the need to hurry, I appreciate how slowly and carefully Cameron is driving right now. I'm sure he is trying to avoid being in an accident on our way to the hospital. He pulls into the drive-through at McDonalds.

"Cameron—Cameron—I think—we may not have time —for this," I pant, holding my belly. The pains are coming much more often now and the baby is pushing against my lower abdomen.

"I'm hungry! It will only take a minute." Cameron flirts with the girl at the window as he picks up his order.

"Cameron—" I repeat through gritted teeth. "I need to get to the hospital."

"Chill out, babe," he says, taking a bite of his breakfast sandwich. "It's only ten minutes away."

When we arrive, I stumble into the waiting room, holding my belly. I try not to groan out loud, but I can't help myself. Cameron tells the nurse on duty that I am in labor. She gets a wheelchair and tells the receptionist to page the doctor, stat. I am in the delivery room and on the bed in less than five minutes. The doctor hurries in and examines me.

"The baby is crowning already. You just made it, my dear," he scolds me.

Cameron sits in a corner of the room. He is on his phone, texting. I wonder if he is contacting his mother to tell her, but I can't ask. The pain consumes me. The nurse holds my hand. I want to scream at her to let go. I don't want anyone touching me. I am angry. It scares me. I grit my teeth, shove my anger back into the recesses of my subconsciousness where it belongs, and take a deep breath.

"Push," I hear someone say, so I do, as hard as I can. I feel the baby slip out and hold my breath as I wait for his cry. He gives a little squeak, then complains more loudly as the nurses rub him briskly with a towel. I see that he has reddish-blonde hair. His skin is pink, not grey like Abigail May's had been, and his arms and legs are flailing as they weigh him. I look over at Cameron. He looks a little pale, but he gives me a smile and a thumbs-up. I am relieved. I've done it right this time.

# Chapter Fifteen

"I can't talk right now." Cameron is whispering into his phone. He thinks I am still asleep. "I just had a baby. I need to focus on that. No. No, I am serious. Just think of it as a break, okay?"

The baby stirs beside me in the bed. We've named him Rowan. I run my hand gently over the top of his soft head and roll over to kiss him. He smells like baby shampoo and powder. It's been three weeks since he was born and I can't get over how lucky I feel. He's a perfect baby. He's already sleeping through most of the night, and he hardly ever cries.

"You're taking time off work?" I ask Cameron.

"Uh, no. Why?" He seems distracted.

"I heard you say you were taking a break."

"Oh, that. Eric wanted to go out for beers this weekend, and I told him no."

"You can go, if you want to. Rowan just mostly eats and sleeps right now." I say that, but I know I will be irritated if Cameron doesn't stay home with me.

"I want to be *here*, with you and Rowan." Cameron smiles

and kisses me tenderly on the mouth. It melts my heart when he does that. I find it difficult to think about anything except how much I love him. I sit up and wrap my arms around his neck.

"Thank you," I whisper in his ear.

He removes my arms from his neck. "Now, I really do have to go to work. I'll be home right after. No meetings today."

"Yay," I say, already thinking about the special dinner I will have waiting for him.

Cameron's phone rings. He's left it on his side of the bed, so I reach over to get it for him. The caller ID says "Kerri." Cameron grabs it from me and presses the "ignore" button. I can see uncertainty in his eyes as he puts the phone in his pocket. He's not sure if I've seen who it is. I pretend I haven't.

"That was Kerri," he says. "She probably wants to tell me something about work. It can wait. No one is allowed to interrupt me when I am saying goodbye to my beautiful wife."

I smile with pleasure. "Goodbye. Have a wonderful day at work. I'll miss you," I tell him.

He kisses me again in that heart-melting way and walks out of the bedroom. I hear the front door open and close. I wait until I hear the car drive away before I go into the room we use as an office and turn on Cameron's computer. He's password protected it, and I can't get in. I only hesitate a minute before calling him. I will get the password somehow. There has to be a way I can do this.

"Hi Cameron. I need to order a few things for Rowan, and I can't get on your computer. Can you please give me the password?"

"Where's your laptop? Use that."

"You know I can only use that for work stuff. I'll get it in trouble if I use it for shopping."

"Well, what do you need? Maybe I can pick it up for you on my way home tonight?"

"Well, I need it now. I was going to use Instacart."

"What could you possibly need today?"

"Um..." I think fast. "Diapers. He has diarrhea and I've had to change him several times this morning. I thought we had extra diapers in the closet but when I went to look, there weren't any. I think I have only two more diapers to last me through the day."

"I'll call my mother. She can bring you some."

"Cameron, that's silly. Just give me the password so I can order them myself."

It's quiet on the other end of the phone. I can almost hear the wheels in his head spinning. *He's trying to come up with an excuse*, I think. *Why?* I can only push so much before he gets angry. This isn't working.

"I'll order them for you when I get to work. You need to rest and not think about these things. I'll take care of you, babe."

"Okay," I say. "Thanks. That's really sweet of you. Pampers. Newborn size."

"No problem. Glad to do it," he says, hanging up.

I take two unopened packages of diapers from Rowan's room and hide them in the laundry bin under the dirty clothes, just in case Cameron looks in the nursery closet when he gets home. I hear Rowan stirring. He'll be awake and hungry in a few minutes so I take a quick shower while I still can.

I am nursing Rowan when the doorbell rings. I press the "talk" button on the Ring camera app. It's Janey with an armful of manila folders.

"Come on in! I'm feeding Rowan."

The door opens, and Janey tiptoes in.

"You don't have to be quiet. He's not sleeping."

Janey comes up behind my chair and puts her finger near Rowan's clenched fist. He opens his hand and then shuts it around her finger. He stops nursing and tries to put her finger in his mouth, his eyes wide open and staring at her.

"What a little cutie," Janey says, cooing at him. I can tell she doesn't want him to let go, but she pries her finger out of his grasp. He starts to cry.

"Sorry, Rowan. You won't get any milk from me!" Janey laughs.

Rowan finds me again and sucks hungrily.

"His little noises sound like humming." Janey says. Maybe he'll be a singer—like you."

"I hope so. I sing to him when Cameron isn't here, so hopefully he'll learn to imitate that."

"What a great idea. They learn talking from us. Why not singing?"

"Exactly," I say, putting Rowan over my shoulder to burp him.

"Anyway," she says, "I brought work for you to do just in case you have time. The boss says you can continue to work from home as long as you need to. He can't afford to lose you. He would never admit that, but it's the truth. I think you and I keep that whole office on track."

"Thanks, Janey. I was worried that Cameron would send me back to work before I am ready. This arrangement is perfect. Please tell Mr. Smithfield I really appreciate it."

"Just keep doing the work, Amelia. He has nothing to complain about."

The tears well up. I can't help it. Janey is a life-saver. I am so grateful.

"I kind of lied to Cameron today," I tell her.

Janey raises an eyebrow. "Go on," she says.

"I told him I needed to order diapers so he would give me his computer password, but I have plenty of them." I'm smiling. I can't help it.

"And did you get the password?"

I shrug. "No. It didn't work. He said he would order diapers for me."

"He's not usually that nice. It sounds a bit suspicious."

"Maybe. Or maybe he really just wants to help me."

"Uh huh." Janey doesn't think that's it, I can tell from the tone of her voice. "Why did you really want the password?"

"I don't know. I just thought—I mean, I wanted to check..."

Janey waits patiently for me to gather my thoughts.

"I overheard a conversation he had on the phone this morning. He thought I was sleeping. I don't know who he was talking to. He said it was Eric, but it didn't sound like a conversation he would have with Eric."

"What did he say?"

"He said something about taking a break."

"What does that mean?"

"I don't know. That's what I wanted to find out."

"Did you ask him about it?"

"Yes. He said he was taking a break from having beers with Eric this weekend."

"And you don't believe him?"

I don't answer right away. I don't want to be disloyal to my husband. I feel a bit guilty that I told Janey anything.

"I don't know," I finally say. "I want to. It makes perfect

sense. I'm just being silly. It must be the postpartum hormones, making me nervous and emotional."

"Maybe," Janey says, frowning. "I've got to get back to work. We'll talk later, okay?"

I nod and put a finger to my lips. Rowan is asleep. Janey tiptoes out the door, closing it gently behind her.

I am on the floor with Rowan, reading him a book, when the doorbell rings about two hours later. It's the Instacart lady with the diapers. I tip her and put the diapers away on the shelf in Rowan's closet where we always keep them. I'm pretty sure Cameron will check. I take two out of the package and hide those with the others in the laundry bin so it looks like I really needed them. It surprises me that I don't feel bad about this. I have never lied to Cameron about anything before.

When Cameron comes home, he goes straight to the closet. "Good! I see they delivered the diapers."

"Yes, thank you. They came around 10:00—just in time."

"Good. So, why is my computer on?"

"I turned it on to order the diapers before I called you. I didn't have the password, so I couldn't shut it down. The screen went dark, so I thought it might already be off anyway. I thought it would be okay even if it wasn't and that you could put in your password and shut it off when you got home. I didn't want to break it."

"Oh, Amelia, that's not how it works." He rolls his eyes. "There's a shut-down button you can access without a password. You'd think you'd be a bit more tech savvy by this point in your life."

"Sorry, it just doesn't interest me," I lie. "I have you for that."

He's pleased. He likes to have me depend on him. He

likes taking care of me. I used to like that, too. Today, it feels a little—restrictive? Controlling? Demeaning? I'm not sure how to describe how I'm feeling. It just feels—not good. I choke back the rising anger and smile at him instead.

"Dinner's almost ready."

Cameron pulls me to him and puts his forehead on mine. "I missed you today."

"You did?" I am surprised to hear him say this. He's not usually so affectionate when he gets home from work.

"Yes, I did." He gives me a kiss. "Now, let's eat before I forget myself and whisk you off to the bedroom."

Rowan passes gas.

"Well, that breaks the mood." Cameron laughs, and I giggle. He picks Rowan up and follows me into the kitchen.

I put dinner on the table and we talk like we used to back in our college days. Cameron seems happy, content, and focused on us. What was I worried about? Silly, silly me.

# Chapter Sixteen

"Happy birthday to you!" Rowan looks at all of us standing around his high chair with confusion and he seems afraid of the lit candle on the cake in front of him. His lips pucker, and I know he is about to cry.

"You're a big boy now," Lorna says, clapping her hands. Laurence stands next to her and joins in the clapping. "Yes, you are. A big, big boy!"

That distracts him and he tries to imitate them by putting his pudgy little hands together. "Bee, bah!" he says.

Eric, Lyla, Mac, and Mac's girlfriend Deirdre ignore everything. They turn away when the song is over and begin pouring themselves drinks from the assortment of liquor Cameron has set out on the counter. I invited Janey, but she is not here. She does not like Cameron's family—or Cameron, either, for that matter. She said she will celebrate with me another time. Maybe we'll take Rowan to the cemetery for a picnic to have cake with his big sister. I've taken him by myself a few times, but he's still too young to understand. He enjoys sitting on the lawn there, pulling up handfuls of grass and throwing them into the wind. When he laughs, I think I hear Abigail May laugh, too. She likes him. They will be good friends, I think.

"Go get ready for your date," Lorna says to me. "I'll give Rowan his bath and get him ready for bed."

I hesitate, but Laurence chimes in, "We've raised two boys. We know what we're doing." He laughs at me. "I know it takes you women a long time to beautify yourselves, so go on now. Cameron doesn't like to be late."

Cameron turns toward me. "I just have to throw on a jacket. I'm all set. We leave in thirty minutes."

He's very excited. We're going to Kerri's house for a small Christmas party with another couple Cameron knows from work. I don't want to go. I don't know these people. I won't know what to say. Cameron will be annoyed with me. I wish I were as outgoing as he is, but I'm not. He knows I'm not. Why is he making me do this? But, I do it anyway, of course. I want to be a good wife, the best wife.

*Stay focused, Amelia,* I tell myself as I sit down on Kerri's sofa. Her husband, Kenny, is across from me in an oversized armchair. He observes me over the rim of his whiskey glass.

"Are you cold, Amelia?" he asks.

"No. No, I'm fine." I uncross my arms and sit up straight. I don't know what to do with my hands. I sit on them, then put them on my lap.

"Would you like a drink, Amelia?"

"Some water, maybe?"

"I'll get that for you." He stands up and walks into the kitchen, where the rest of the people are. I hear Cameron say something that makes Kerri and her friend laugh as they prepare the meal. Kenny doesn't come back right away. I am alone in this strange house. They have forgotten me already.

I should probably get up and join them—Cameron would want me to—but I don't.

Kerri comes out of the kitchen. She is holding Cameron's hands, pulling him along behind her. They don't see me at first.

"Oh!" Kerri drops Cameron's hands.

"Kerri's showing me the house," Cameron says. "Why don't you join the others in the kitchen—be sociable." He sounds a bit annoyed.

I watch as they walk down the hallway toward the other end of the house. I stay exactly where I am on the couch. I don't want to be by myself with these strangers. I check my watch. Ten minutes. Twelve minutes. Cameron and Kerri don't come back. Is there another way to the kitchen from wherever they went?

I take a deep breath and stand up. Kenny calls from the kitchen, "It's time to eat!" I follow his voice and find the dining room on the other side of the kitchen. Cameron comes up behind me and pulls out a chair.

"Here you go, babe," he says.

"Where's Kerri?" Kenny asks.

"I have no idea," Cameron says. "She showed me a bit of the house and then said she was going to the bathroom. I haven't seen her in a while."

Kerri comes in. "Sorry, everyone. A bit of a stomach ache. I'm good now! Thanks, Josie, for getting everything on the table. What would I do without you?" Kerri gives her friend a kiss on the cheek and winks at her.

Josie's husband, Victor, sits at one end of the table. Kenny sits at the other. Cameron and I are seated next to each other, across from Kerri and Josie. They all chat happily while we eat. Only Kenny and I are quiet. He's not saying much either, just drinking a lot. After dinner, we

Cheryl Thomas

play a game of Trivial Pursuit, each couple a team. I manage to get the last one right and win the game for us. Cameron is surprised.

"How did you know that answer?" he asks on the way home.

I shrug. "A lucky guess?"

"Hmmm." He agrees. It has to be a lucky guess. He doesn't think I know much about anything. "Did you have a good time tonight?"

I did not. I think his friends are rude and self-centered. "It was interesting," I tell him. "Did you?"

"Did I what?" We pull into the driveway.

"Did you have a good time?"

He looks at me sideways. "Of course. My friends are great. It was a good opportunity to meet the spouses and get to know them a little bit. I wish you had been friendlier. They think you're a snob."

"Did they say that?"

"No, but I could tell. They tried to talk to you, but you gave one-word answers like you didn't really want to be there."

"I didn't want to be there."

"Well, so sorry that I have friends and that I like to have fun," Cameron says snidely. He's angry with me again.

"You know I'm uncomfortable in situations where I don't know anyone and that I prefer to just listen and be in the background. I've never told you that you have to be the same way. I love that you are so outgoing and friendly."

"Your behavior reflects badly on me. I shouldn't always have to make excuses for you, Amelia. You'll never get to know them and be comfortable with them if you don't try. For Pete's sake, how hard is it to smile and talk to people?"

Hard. Very hard—for me. But I don't say that. "You're

right, Cameron. It's not that difficult. I was a jerk tonight. I'm sorry. I'll do better." I try to keep the resentment at bay. He knew who I was when he married me. Why are we doing this?

He gets out and slams the car door. I stay in my seat until he goes into the house. Then, I get out and slam my door as hard as I can. That actually feels good. I open it and slam it again.

Lorna and Laurence come out through the garage. "Rowan was as good as gold, Amelia," Lorna tells me. "He's sound asleep."

"Thank you, Lorna."

"Anytime," she says, kissing me on the cheek.

Laurence looks like he wants to ask me something. He hesitates for a moment, then just says, "Good night, Amelia."

"Goodnight." I want to slam the car door again, but they are watching me. I go into the house and push the remote button that closes the garage door. It slides down, and they slowly disappear from view.

# Chapter Seventeen

It's Valentine's Day and Cameron's band will be playing for a big party at the American Legion Hall tonight.

"You can come if you want to, Amelia," he tells me. "But it's all old people who come to hold hands and dance with other eighty-year-olds."

"I'll stay home with Rowan, thank you." I smile at him. "We can celebrate when you get home." I hold up sexy lingerie I have saved for the occasion.

Cameron laughs. "I'll be home as fast as I can. Oh, I have a present for you."

He hands me a small box wrapped in red paper. It's a clear plastic figurine of a teddy bear holding a red heart.

"Thank you, Cameron. It's very cute!"

"You're welcome. Now, I've got to get ready."

He goes in to the bathroom and turns on the shower. His phone pings. It's a message from Kerri. I pick up the phone. I don't have his password, so I can only see the first few lines in the notification. "Hi darling," it says. "I know you said not to text, but I can't wait to feel your arms..."

I put the phone back on the bedside table and leave the room. My hands are shaking.

"Was that my phone?" Cameron comes out of the bathroom, still wet.

"What?" I ask, coming back to the bedroom doorway.

"My phone. Did my phone ring? Where's my phone?"

"I don't know," I tell him. "I was in the nursery checking on Rowan. He should be up from his afternoon nap soon. Do you want me to check?"

"Ah, here it is." He picks up his phone. "Oh, just a spam message. I thought it might be Victor with information about tonight." He takes the phone with him back into the bathroom, and I hear the click of the door being locked.

I will give him the benefit of the doubt. There is no need to worry. Kerri probably thought she was talking to her husband and dialed Cameron by mistake. How embarrassing for her. And Cameron just needs his phone with him in the bathroom to text Victor to confirm details for tonight's performance, like he said.

I go in to the office and pack up the laptop I use for work. I take it to the kitchen and hide it under the sink behind all of the cleaning products. Then, I go outside and ring our doorbell. I walk to the office and then back to the living room. I open the front door and close it. "Goodbye! Thanks!" I say to no one.

"Who was that?" Cameron comes out of the bedroom, still wrapped in a towel.

"Oh, just Janey," I say. "She said our laptops need an update and she was told to come collect mine. She'll bring it back tomorrow after work."

"Odd that she didn't stay and chat," he says suspiciously. "Janey loves to talk."

"Oh, she was in a hurry to get to church. She always

goes to her Sunday evening service, you know. I'm sure she'll stay for a long chat when she brings the laptop back. Shall we invite her for dinner tomorrow then?"

"Sure. Whatever you want." Cameron goes back into the bedroom to finish getting ready.

I am playing with Rowan on the living room floor when Cameron comes out to put on his coat.

"Cameron, I need your help," I say.

"Now?" he asks impatiently. "I've got to go."

"Please?" I force tears into my eyes. "I have a project I was supposed to finish by tomorrow morning, and I forgot all about it. I'm such a ditz."

"So? Finish it."

"I—I need a computer."

He looks at me, not understanding.

"Janey has my laptop. Can I please use yours? Just for tonight? You can sign on for me—you don't need to give me your password—and I'll sign out just as soon as I'm done. I promise! You can show me how."

"No. You should have thought about this before." He shrugs as if he just doesn't care.

"But, Cameron, I'll get fired. We need the money! Please!"

He hesitates. He likes having my money. I pick up Rowan and follow Cameron into the office. I stand behind him and watch as he types in "R-O-w-A-n." The computer comes to life. I turn around so my back is to Cameron and bounce Rowan on my hip. He's getting restless and is letting me know he does not want to be held.

"You're all set," Cameron says, turning around to see if I'm watching him. "To shut it down, just do this." He shows me a series of keystrokes, then sighs. "I'll write it down for you so you remember."

"Thank you." I put Rowan in the playpen with his toys and pick up a manilla folder. "You're my knight in shining armor." I smile sweetly at Cameron and give him a kiss.

"You're welcome." He looks nervous but doesn't say anything more. He has to go now or be late. He jots down the information I need to shut down the computer and hurries out the door.

I wait until I hear the garage door close and the car drive away before I begin searching his computer files. There are dozens of emails to and from Kerri. I open one of them.

*"My darling Kerri, thanks for spending your lunchtime with me today. We do not have many left this year, depending on how the schedule shakes out, but even if I'm teaching, you could have lunch in my room (no – on second thought, I would be WAY too distracted to carry on with the lesson). But I really enjoyed hearing your stories, especially about the Catholic school. It was easy to envision you doing all of those things as you were telling them to me, and I'm smiling now remembering them. Funny, but an old song just popped into my head. Are you familiar with 'I Get a Kick Out of You'? I DO get such a kick out of you – everything about you. Every time I see you I think how incredibly special you are. And just when I think I've got you figured out, you surprise me— like the jewelry design! But I should have known that someone so creative would have multiple ways of expressing it. As I write this, there is so much I feel I want to say, but they're things that need to be shared in person, without pressures of time or location, which always seem to interfere. There are times when I think that we've said it all again and again, and that we understand each other well; but there are*

*other times when I think we've only begun to scratch the surface of trying to figure out what it is that we seem to have stumbled into. What do you think? I will miss not seeing you or hearing your voice this weekend. Be safe, and know that I'm thinking about you. See you Monday. AYW."*

I am unfamiliar with anyone who could be AYW. Those are not Cameron's initials. I breathe a sigh of relief. He must be allowing someone else at work to use his email. That has to be the explanation. But why? And those are not Kerri's husband's initials, either. Is Cameron covering for her? I notice there is a response sent a few days later, and open it.

*"My dear Cameron, you wrote: 'There are times when I think that we've said it all again and again, and that we under-stand each other well; but there are other times when I think we've only begun to scratch the surface of trying to figure out what it is that we seem to have stumbled into. I think that if I spent the rest of my lifetime trying to figure this out, I still wouldn't be able to. I also don't know if it can be, or needs to be, figured out. What I do know is that you are always on my mind. Sitting in traffic yesterday, I spent my time looking at my reflection in the rearview mirror, and I kept pretending that I was looking at you—WISHING I was looking at you. This morning, I turned on the TV and I was wishing you were lying next to me in bed watching with me. I just wanted to be lying next to you not saying anything at all. Anyway, to further distract myself until Monday morning comes, I'm going to do a load of boring, yet necessary, errands —one of which is getting my girly nails done. I banged my left middle finger this morning and the whole fake nail*

*popped off (yes, OUCH!). I have to decide whether to replace it, or just get them all taken off and let the real ones start living again. Such important decisions to make! I've gotten used to them and you can't (or maybe you can) imagine how pathetically ugly the real nail looks. I'll try to check my email again this weekend, but have no idea if I'll be able to without Kenny being suspicious. I think the library will be open on Sundays now that school has started, so maybe I can check from there. Missing you. —Kerri."*

The evidence is hard to ignore. I would like to, though. Ignore everything and just go back to living in my own, perfect world. I feel myself slipping into oblivion but the anger bubbling underneath stops me.

I search the internet for a spyware program that will let me access Cameron's account from my own computer and install it. I check my watch. There's plenty of time yet before Cameron comes home. Rowan has fallen asleep in the playpen. I open the next email.

*"I wasn't sure when you would get my previous email, but I'm glad you got it, and I'm glad you were able to respond. So what did you bang your middle finger on that it ripped the nail off? I assume you've made your important decision regarding whether to fix it or rip them all off. Either way, you have beautiful hands...very kissable, you know ;-) I thought about you all day—looked at your picture on my phone quite a number of times, and wanted to be wherever you were. One of my daydreams had you doing a cartwheel right into my arms. Think you could pull that off? Thinking, wishing, and hoping is all well and good, but like the song says, 'Ain't*

*nothin' like the real thing', so I'll be looking forward to Monday morning. See you then. Cameron."*

I struggle not to slam the cover of the laptop shut. I don't want to know. I close my eyes and take a deep breath. I need to know. I imagine this is happening to someone else. It's a story, not real life. It's a dream, a nightmare that will be over soon.

*"Kerri, I know that with the birthday celebration, you probably won't see this until morning, but I wanted to jot some things down that have been rambling around in my head since this afternoon. One—Thank you for the chili. It was really excellent. So, the chicken soup and the chocolate chip cookies were not exceptions, but the rule! I had a hard enough time when I came to the realization that I had fallen in love with someone who votes Democrat, but being in love with a woman who cooks better than I do? That's going to take a great deal of adjustment."*

What is he talking about? He doesn't cook. At least, not for me. Now I have doubts again that this is my Cameron. Perhaps it's a different one. Or maybe he's using Cameron's name so Kenny doesn't find out Kerri is having an affair. Emails from a coworker wouldn't look as suspicious, would they? I swallow and continue reading.

*"Two—You DO realize that I want to spend every possible moment with you, right? If I walk in a different direction, it's*

*just because I either think you need time to yourself or I don't want to give tongues an opportunity to wag. If you need me, all you have to do is call. I'll be there. I hope you know that by now. Three—I hope you don't think I laughed too hard when I gave you the tomatoes in the Victoria's Secret box this afternoon. I wasn't trying to be cruel, just funny. The look on your face was a mixture of shock, maybe a little happiness, some panic, and—what's an adjective which would convey 'O my GOD, WHAT has this nut done now?' I can't wait to see the look on your face when I really get you something from that store. Four—Thank you for not sitting behind me at the meeting today. It was much nicer to just be able to look up and see you whenever I wanted to. I think that should be your assigned seat, unless you want to find one closer. I'll save the rest for dinner tomorrow. Think about what kind of food you'd like, and I'll see you in the morning. Cameron"*

So, where did Kerri think Cameron got the Victoria's Secret box? The contents of that box—the real contents—had been a present for me. At least, I thought so at the time. I feel sick, remembering how I modeled it for him before we made love. He had seemed extra passionate that night. I thought it was the lingerie that sparked his interest in me again, but now I think it was because he was imagining a different partner, making love to her. I had been simply a body. I am not unfamiliar with the anger rising in me, but it is becoming more and more difficult to push it back into its box as I continue reading.

. . .

*"Just so you know, we're even-steven. I killed you yesterday with the unmentionables, and you killed me today when you said Amelia should send me a thank-you card because I am the one who gets you erect, but she gets to enjoy it. Even though I got the reference right then and there, it sort of had a sunburn effect. It's like you know you have one, but it doesn't start to really hurt until hours later, like when you're trying to fall asleep. I call a truce. I think we know darn well enough how we feel—no need to exemplify it anymore. Love, Kerri."*

*"Kerri, I'm so sorry. It wasn't intended to hurt or to get even. I'm not even going to try and explain it here for fear of making it worse, but PLEASE know I didn't say it to hurt you. Amid all of the stress laid upon us these last two weeks, you have been, and continue to be, THE bright spot in every day for me. As you wish, Cameron.*

AYW. As you wish. Ah, there it is. It's a quote from *The Princess Bride*. Buttercup's one true love. Does he really imagine he is that? I want to laugh, to feel anything, actually, but I'm numb.

*"I know that you weren't intending to hurt me – and it didn't really. It made me jealous in a way that I have no right to be, but still feel, so don't think I'm mad or upset or anything like that. Just longing for something I can't have. As you wish yourself! —Kerri."*

.   .   .

*"I loved getting your text message. To be reminded that you're thinking about me out of the blue like that just...well you could just knock me down with a feather, to use an over-used cliché. I never know when I can text back—if you'll be alone—so I usually take the safe approach and just sit here and 'glow' (at least that's what it feels like), hoping that you understand that I'm thinking of you, too. I was missing you so badly this morning it felt like the summer when I can't see you everyday—so I started a little project to console myself (you'll see on Monday). But your text message and emails have brought a huge smile to my face. Talk to you soon! — Cameron."*

*"I'm so glad my text message brought a smile and glow to your day. You know I wish I could make you glow 24/7. I generally don't text you unless I am alone, but you did the wise thing and waited. —Kerri."*

*"It's 7:00 a.m. on Friday. I'm sitting here alone and all I can think about is you. I want to be wherever you are—right next to you, right now. Rather than sit here and be miserable because I can't be with you, I started to think about all of the things that make me happy and began writing them down. Anyway, this list is by no means complete, but here's what I've got so far, in no particular order—*

- *Listening to music with you*
- *Sharing a piece of cheesecake with you*
- *Finding a recipe and MAKING cheesecake for you*
- *Looking into your eyes*

- *Walking past your classroom and seeing you see me*
- *Thinking about you*
- *Dreaming about you*
- *Getting you fries*
- *Getting you coffee*
- *Looking at your picture on my phone*
- *Looking at your picture on my computer desktop*
- *Looking at you*
- *Holding you*
- *Kissing your hand*
- *Kissing your neck*
- *Kissing your lips*
- *Kissing any other part of you*
- *Watching TV with you*
- *Getting an email from you*
- *Getting a card from you*
- *Getting a note from you*
- *Reading your emails, cards and notes over and over again*
- *Writing to you*
- *Talking with you*
- *Listening to you*
- *Making you smile*
- *Making you laugh*
- *Thinking up new ways to make you smile and laugh*
- *Having dinner with you*
- *Having lunch with you*
- *Having breakfast with you*
- *Having breakfast, lunch and dinner with you all in the same day*

## Crazy in Love

- Holding your hand and taking a walk in the moonlight with you
- Lifting you off the ground and cradling you in my arms with your arms around my neck
- Buying you roses
- Drawing a rose softly across your skin
- Standing in the back of your room watching a movie, and having you lean up against me like you just want to stay there forever.
- Sitting next to you at a table full of people and feeling you touch my hand under the table
- Sitting next to you at a table full of people and feeling your toes in the side of my shoe
- Laughing at an inside joke with you
- Making an inside joke and having you look at me strangely because you don't remember
- Sitting in a restaurant alone with you
- Sitting BEHIND a restaurant alone with you
- Taking long car rides with you
- Playing the piano for you
- Getting a text message from you
- Seeing your name on my caller ID
- Having you come into my classroom unexpectedly
- Having you come into my classroom first thing in the morning and walk straight over to kiss me
- Cooking for you
- Eating something you've cooked
- Getting drenched in the pouring rain while getting a turkey sandwich for you
- Telling you I love you
- Hearing you say 'I love you'

*Have you found the common thread? A word that's in every single sentence? YOU make me happy!"*

I can't help myself. I run to the bathroom and kneel in front of the toilet. It's just dry heaves—I haven't eaten all day—but I can't stop. This has obviously been going on for a long time. How have I missed it?

# Chapter Eighteen

It's 5:00 in the morning. I know that because I have been staring at the clock all night. I hear the front door open and close, and then Cameron's soft footsteps as he tiptoes into our bedroom. I close my eyes and pretend to be asleep. He slides silently into bed and slowly pulls the sheets up to cover himself. I do not stir. I hear him sigh with relief as he turns away from me. I wait an hour before I get out of bed and go into the bathroom. I flick on the bedroom lights when I come back and don't even try to be quiet.

"Amelia! I'm trying to sleep!" Cameron pulls the covers over his head.

"There's something I have to ask you about before Rowan wakes up." I walk over to the chair near his side of the bed and turn it so that it is facing him and close, so close, to where his head is. I sit and stare at him.

"What is it?" Cameron removes the sheet from his head and stares back.

"I think you know."

He doesn't speak for about a minute. He just stares back

at me. I can almost see the wheels turning in his head as he searches for what to say.

"I *don't* know, Amelia. Can you please stop being so cryptic and just tell me what's on your mind? Geez. I hate when you do this. You always imagine things that never turn out to be real."

"I saw the emails, Cameron."

"What emails are you talking about? For Pete's sake, I've had a long night and very little sleep. Just get to the point or leave me alone."

"The emails you and Kerri sent to each other."

He doesn't answer right away so I know he is thinking about what I've said. I am expecting him to deny it, but instead he finally says, "Yeah? I figured you would find them when I let you use my computer. You are the nosiest person I've ever met. They are none of your business, Amelia. Those are private."

"If you are having an affair, it *is* my business. I'm your wife!"

"It was just a little harmless flirting. This is what I mean, Amelia. You take something innocent and make it out to be a terrible thing." He sits up and puts his legs over the bed so he is facing me now. He takes my hands in his. "Amelia, my darling, I think you have a problem—a mental problem. This is not the way a normal person would interpret those emails. Shall I call Dr. Gherhart and set up an appointment for you? I'm really worried."

Dr. Gherhart is a psychiatrist I met with a few times in the past—a very long time ago actually—after my mother died. I was just a teenager and my father took me to Dr. Gherhart to "help you deal with the situation," he told me. I'm not sure how Cameron knows that. Maybe I told him. I can't remember. My head is starting to hurt.

"No. No, I'm okay. It's just—they sounded like—you kissed her?" Maybe I *am* wrong. Maybe I'm not seeing things clearly.

Cameron laughs. "Just harmless flirting, babe. I never kissed her. I would never kiss her. Anyway, we don't flirt anymore. We're just friends."

"Oh." I don't know what else to say. My mind is blank. I feel the darkness coming and fight it.

"Now, if that's all, I think I hear Rowan. You'd better go get him. Maybe a walk to the park would do you both good this morning?"

I feel like a robot as I dress Rowan and make breakfast for all of us. Cameron watches me as I put on a coat and wrap Rowan warmly in his stroller. "We'll be back in about an hour," I tell Cameron. "We're going to the park."

"Good," he says, giving me a hug. "I think it's exactly what you need."

I head out the door, but hesitate just long enough to glance back at Cameron. He's hurrying to the office, and I know those emails will be gone before I get back. It doesn't matter, though. I can check every keystroke he makes with the spyware I installed. If he writes to her again, I will see it. I will know.

I push the stroller toward the park. Although the sidewalks have been cleared of snow, it is still difficult to manage. Rowan seems to be enjoying it, though, so I keep going. A car pulls up next to me.

"Amelia, whatever are you doing?" It is Lorna. "It is much too cold to have the baby outside! Get in the car."

She puts Rowan in the carseat while I fold up the stroller and put it in the trunk. I get in the front seat and shut the door.

"Where were you going? Why didn't you drive? Is

something wrong with your car?" Her questions are giving me another headache.

"I was just taking Rowan to the park."

"It has to be below freezing out there! What were you thinking?"

"It's actually thirty-seven degrees and I wrapped him up with lots of blankets, so I don't think he's cold. He liked it."

"Well, I won't have it. I'm taking you home."

"Cameron won't like that."

"Why not? Does he know you are out here, in the freezing cold, with the baby?"

"He actually suggested it." I am feeling petulant but I get in the front next to Lorna anyway. I'm tired of being blamed for everything. "We had a fight, and he thought it would be helpful for me to get some fresh air."

"Oh dear. A fight about what?" Lorna squints at me with concern as she puts the car in drive and heads back down the road toward my house.

I hesitate. Cameron said it was private, so I'm not sure if I should say anything, but I do anyway. "He was flirting with Kerri, and I thought he was having an affair."

"Heavens, Amelia! Cameron would never do that! He would never jeopardize your marriage. Divorce is a huge taboo in our family. A widower—or widow—is viewed with respect and compassion. One cannot help that. But divorce is the same as failure! All of society would frown on that. Yes. They would definitely frown on that." She is upset. "You are not thinking of divorce, are you, Amelia?"

"No," I tell her. "Cameron says it was just harmless flirting. He's not doing it anymore."

"Of course not." Lorna pulls into my driveway and shuts the car off. "Now, let's go see what this is all about."

"Cameron? Cameron?" Lorna calls out to him as we go into the house. "What's this I hear about flirting?"

Cameron narrows his eyes and scowls at me. "What did she tell you?"

"That you have been flirting a bit with a coworker. That has to stop, Cameron."

"I'm just on my way into the kitchen for some coffee," he tells her. "Come help me. I'll make you a cup too."

I have to change Rowan's diaper, so I can't follow them, but I wait just a minute outside the door where I can listen.

"There's something wrong with her, Mom," I hear Cameron say. "I didn't do anything, but she's making it seem like I did. There are no emails, there was no flirting. There's absolutely nothing going on between me and Kerri. She's making all this stuff up, and it scares me. I'm concerned about her."

"Oh, Cameron, you're such a sweetheart. Of course, you're concerned. I am, too, now that you've told me. We've got to get her to the doctor."

"I'm calling her psychiatrist to set up an appointment this morning."

"Oh my. She has a *psychiatrist*?" Lorna raises her eyebrows in surprise.

"Yes. I didn't want to say anything, Mom. I thought she was better, but now I'm not sure that my loving her is enough to fix things. I've tried, Mom. I've really tried."

"Now, Cameron. A mental problem is an *illness*. You can't abandon her for that. You're not thinking about divorce, surely."

"Of course not, Mom. I promised to be hers in sickness and in health, until death do us part, and I meant it. We'll get through this."

Their voices fade away as I walk toward the nursery. "I

am not crazy," I tell Rowan. He smiles at me and laughs as if I have just said the funniest thing ever. "I bet he's deleted all of the emails so there's no evidence. What do you think?" I lay him down on the changing table.

Rowan claps his hands, then puts them over his eyes. He takes them away. "Boo!" he says, laughing.

"Peek-a-boo to you!" I answer him, tickling his belly.

"Down!" he demands. I finish changing his diaper and put him on the floor with his toys.

When I go back to the living room, Cameron and his mother are drinking their coffee as if nothing has happened.

"Where's Rowan?" Lorna asks me.

"He's in his room, playing."

"By himself? Shouldn't he be supervised?"

"He's fine."

I see her exchange a worried glance with Cameron and feel like I need to explain.

"I can see the door to his room from where I am sitting. He'll crawl out here in a few minutes. I like for him to be able to entertain himself, to be a bit independent whenever possible. He will come searching for us when he gets bored."

I have no sooner said this than Lora points to the nursery door. "Look! He's standing by himself! Big boy! Big boy," she coos at him. "Come to Grandma!" Lorna holds out her hands and Rowan lets go of the wall. He takes two steps toward her before he falls on his bottom.

"Did you see that? His very first steps! And they were to Grandma!" She is very excited. I've seen him do it before, but I don't want to burst her bubble. She can have this moment.

"That made my day," she says. "I really have to go, but I

am thrilled I was here to witness that! I can't wait to tell Laurence!"

Lorna gives me a kiss on the cheek before she leaves and pats my back. "I'll be praying for you, my dear. You'll be all right."

Cameron shrugs and looks at me as if to say, "I have no idea what she's talking about," but I know that he does.

# Chapter Nineteen

I haven't checked the spyware since I installed it three months ago. I'm feeling silly now about doing that. Cameron has been very attentive. He comes home every night and we play with Rowan until his bedtime, have dinner together, and even make love a couple of times a week. Life couldn't be more perfect. Maybe I really did imagine the whole email thing. Cameron hasn't said anything about it or about my going to the psychiatrist again. I hope he's forgotten. Or maybe I imagined that too.

"Cameron?" He's sitting on the couch having a beer, waiting for me to finish the dishes so we can watch a movie together.

"What's up, babe?" He smiles up at me and pats the cushion next to him.

"I've been thinking about those emails." I hold up a hand to stop him from interrupting me. He looks annoyed. "I think you may be right about me imagining them. Can you show me? Just so I know for sure it was just all in my head? That it's not real?"

"I can if you really want me to, but I don't know if that's

a good idea, Amelia. I don't want to trigger another episode."

"I'm ready, Cameron. I need to know. I want to trust you. I do trust you. It's just that…"

Cameron shrugs and gets up. "Come on," he says as he walks toward our home office. He turns on the computer and opens his email. There are two old emails from Kerri. He opens the first one. I lean over his shoulder to see what it says.

"Put on your glasses, Amelia. It's annoying when you lean on me."

I put on my glasses and read the email out loud. "Cameron, I have a student that wants to take voice lessons on Tuesdays after school. Can you fit her into your schedule?"

"Okay?" says Cameron. "Shall I open the next one?" I nod.

"Cameron," it says. "This is a reminder of the faculty meeting on Friday from 4:00 to 6:00 pm. The principal expects us to come prepared to share ideas about how we can all communicate better."

"Thanks, Cameron." The emails really were just about work. "I'm not sure why I was so upset." I rub away the tear rolling down my cheek. I feel confused and broken. What is wrong with me? Maybe I do need to talk to Dr. Gherhart.

"You did that in-your-own-head thing again. That has to stop, Amelia."

"I'm sorry," I say.

"Just stop doing it," Cameron says. "You don't have anything to worry about."

"Okay," I say. I'm embarrassed. "Let's go watch our movie now."

I don't even know what movie we are watching. My

mind is reeling and I can't pay attention. I was so sure about those emails, but the ones I just read are certainly not romantic or suggestive like the ones I thought I had seen before, the ones that have vanished. Or, perhaps, they really never *were* there. It scares me. I have always retreated into my mind to escape the bad things, not to create them. What is happening to me? I rest my head on Cameron's shoulder for the remainder of the movie. I am lucky he is so patient and kind. What other man would put up with this? With me?

In the morning, I scatter Rowan's toys around me in the living room and put him down to play with them. He likes to be with me while I work. I turn on my computer and open one of the files Janey has sent for me to untangle. I *intend* to forget about the emails. I *want* to forget about them, but something tickles the back of my mind, so I close the file from work and click on the spyware application instead. I have to see the emails one more time. Just to be sure.

It opens and offers me a view of all of Cameron's emails. There's nothing there except what I saw this morning. He's telling the truth. I am just about to shut it down, relieved, when I notice the keystroke file. It blinks at me. I stare at it for a minute, then open it. Much of it is gibberish, as if he's typed, then backspaced, then typed and backspaced again, but I can make out certain words. Love. Miss you. Be careful. Use code. Hahahaha. See you at the diner. Vibrator. Fun.

I can't read anymore. I shut the laptop and curl up on the couch, hugging my knees. I don't know what this means. I am having trouble processing any of it.

Rowan toddles over to the couch, and touches my face.

"Ba-ba?" he says. "Boo-ba?" He tries to give me one of the plastic dinosaurs he has carried over in his two fists. "Rrrrr!" He growls as if he is the dinosaur.

I uncurl myself and sit on the floor with him. I take the dinosaur he's offering me. "Rrrrr!" I growl back. It comes out a little louder than I intended, but Rowan likes it. He laughs as we make our dinosaurs stomp up and down my crisscrossed legs and across my lap.

There is a knock at the front door and Janey comes in. "Hello!" she calls. "The boss gave me permission to come by and see how you're doing. I haven't heard much from you for a few weeks."

"Oh. I've turned in most of the work you sent me. I just have a few more projects to go."

"I'm not really asking about work, sweetie. I'm asking about you!" She picks Rowan up and blows raspberries on his belly. He loves the attention, so he doesn't mind that our playtime has been interrupted.

I just shrug. "Would you like a cup of coffee?"

"Sure," she says. She follows me into the kitchen, still holding Rowan. She chatters a bit about the people at work while I put a k-cup in the coffee maker, and informs me that she had a visit from her son last week, so that's why she hasn't been over sooner.

"How's he doing?" I ask her.

"Oh, he's great! He's finishing up a class in cyber security. It sounds interesting. The class had to hack computers so they learn how to defend against real hackers. One of his assignments was to send out phishing emails to see if anyone would open them and that's how he was able to get into their computer. No one in the class did actual damage to anyone, of course, but they learned a lot about techniques and how to keep computers and apps safe from these kinds of things."

"It sounds interesting." It doesn't really, but Janey is my friend, so I want to listen.

"He wants to work for the FBI in the cybercrime department and—"

"Janey?" I interrupt her. She looks at me expectantly, a bit surprised. "Would your son be able to recover something, like an email, that had been erased—I mean, deleted?"

"Oh, I'm sure he would. Why?"

"I thought I saw some emails in Cameron's account from a woman he works with, but he said I was just imagining it. When I insisted that I really did see them, he showed me his account and they weren't there anymore. I need to know if he deleted them or if I really am crazy. I *feel* crazy. I'm scared, Janey. I don't want to be put into a psych hospital."

Rowan yawns and puts his head down on Janey's shoulder. "Let me put Rowan down for a nap and then we'll talk," she says. Her calm demeanor diminishes my anxiety only slightly.

My hands shake as I pick up my coffee cup. I look into the dark liquid and see my mother. She is wearing jeans and a coffee-colored sweater. I close my eyes and feel its softness and its warmth against my cheek when I hug her goodbye. She doesn't struggle as strange men with serious expressions on their faces put a straightjacket on her. She looks at me with fear in her eyes. At first, I think she is afraid for herself, but then I realize she is afraid for me. She is not looking at me, though. She is looking at the man standing behind me, with his hands on my shoulders. She is looking at my father.

"Amelia? Amelia?" I hear the voice, but I can't focus. A

hand on my arm brings me back to the present. "Amelia! Are you all right?"

"Oh, sorry, Janey. I was just thinking about—something. Here's your coffee." I hand her a full mug and sit down at the kitchen table. She pulls out a chair and sits across from me.

"What is going on? Spill it."

"I thought Cameron was having an affair with Kerri. You know, the woman he works with at the Bach Academy." It sounds silly when I say it out loud. Cameron loves me. He would never do that.

"There must be a reason you thought that." Janey encourages me to keep talking.

"Oh, now that I think about it, it's just me being moody, I guess. I'm tired from working and taking care of the house and the baby—"

"Nope." Janey reaches across the table and takes my hands in hers. "I don't believe that. Tell me everything."

I hesitate. "Well, I found suggestive emails to and from Kerri on Cameron's computer. Or, at least, I thought I did. I confronted Cameron about it, and he told me it was just harmless flirting, but later he told his mother they were work emails, that he and Kerri are co-workers and friends, nothing more. When I asked him to show me the emails again, he was right. There were two emails from Kerri, and both were about work things."

"So? He could have deleted the other ones."

"I would like to know that for sure. He says he didn't delete anything, but I don't know how to check that. I put spyware on his computer—"

"What? You did? Clever you!" She is grinning from ear to ear. "What did you find out?"

"There were no suggestive emails but I don't think the

spyware can tell me if he deleted anything. It only shows me what's there. I can also see keystrokes of what he's typed, but, if he did write emails to Kerri, it must have been before I installed the spyware because I didn't see anything that resembled what I read."

"Let's have a look, shall we? My son has shown me a few things. I might be able to figure this out."

I'm startled. "You believe me? You don't think I'm— crazy?"

"Of course not! You're one of the sanest people I know. If you say the email was there, it was there."

"If you can find it—that means I'm not imagining things, seeing things that aren't there." *Like my mother*, I think.

"Your mother imagines a lot of things that never happened," my father told me when I was about sixteen. "She even accused me of trying to kill her a couple of times. She isn't right in the head, Amelia. I had no choice but to send her to a psychiatric hospital for a while."

When my mother came home from the hospital a year later, she was different. Quieter. She never imagined anything again up to the day she died, or at least she never spoke of it if she did. How *did* she die? For the life of me, I can't remember.

I go get my laptop and open the spyware program.

"This is amazing!" Janey says as she gets to work.

It doesn't take her long to find the "deleted files" folder. She grins up at me and clicks on the icon. Dozens of emails from the past few years scroll down. They aren't all about Kerri, but I want to see those that are before looking at anything else. Janey opens one.

"Ha! I knew it!" I'm so relieved. I didn't imagine any of it. Here they are, right in front of me. "Wait! Janey—can you—can you see them too? I'm not making this up, am I?"

"You are not, my girl. He's guilty as sin." She hits the print button. "I'm taking the proof home with me to keep it safe. There are more. Do you want to see them, too?"

I nod. I am glad she is here as a witness. She clicks on the oldest one she can find. It's from May, two years ago. "Let's start at the beginning, shall we?"

# Chapter Twenty

I'm putting together a timeline of Cameron's activities so I can start to make sense of everything. It's helping me stay numb enough to function normally each day. I really don't know what else to do.

"Did he ever love me?" I ask Janey as we pour over some of the emails from Cameron's account. I read them several times. The words don't make sense to me.

"I don't know, sweetie," she says.

"I am unlovable. There's nothing about me that anyone could love."

"That is not true. I love you." Janey puts her hand on mine and squeezes gently.

"You don't count." I can see that I've offended her. "Sorry. I don't mean that in a bad way. You're like a mother to me, and so of course you would love me. I love you, too. It's a different kind of love than a husband and wife should have, though. Isn't it?"

"I get it. I really do. Everyone needs to be the 'one and only' of someone else, to be the most important person in his or her life."

I can't speak through my tears, so I just nod. The only thing on my timeline so far is the date of our marriage and the words: Cameron promised to love and cherish me until death do us part.

"He went to a Broadway show with Kerri in May," Janey informs me. "Two years ago." I add that to the timeline. How had I not known that? Why didn't he take *me*?

"I don't know if I can do this, Janey." I put down my pen.

"If you want to stop, we'll stop," she says. "But I think it might be best for you to know the actual truth, not what Cameron pretends is the truth."

"I'm not crazy," I whisper.

"No, sweetie, you're not crazy. I think the only crazy one here is Cameron. He's crazy for doing this to you, for risking his reputation and his family. You won't stay with him once we collect all the evidence, will you Amelia?"

I don't answer. Instead, I pick up my pen. "What happened next?" I ask her.

Janey sighs. "Well, I can see that Cameron communicates with women on all kinds of porn sites on a regular basis. There's a lot of kinky stuff here you don't need to read. I'll just print it all out and put it with the rest of the evidence."

"He does that during the same time he's pursuing Kerri? The same time he is supposedly falling in love with her? When he was making love to me?" I feel the anger pushing hard against the walls I have built to keep it at bay.

"Yep. What a great guy." She says yes, but she is shaking her head no.

"I don't—"

"Whoa!" Janey suddenly sits up straight. "Evidently Kerri told him not to contact her, that she couldn't look at herself in the mirror because of the secret relationship they started five weeks ago—that would have been the May thing, I think. This email is dated June 14th. His response is that he truly loves her and would run back to her in a minute even though he knows what they are doing is wrong. He says he will never regret what happened between them. He told her she is the only woman—besides you—for whom he has had feelings and he doesn't want what happened between them to damage their friendship. Etcetera, etcetera."

"He has feelings for me? So he's just confused, then. He'll figure it out and come around." I feel elated. There's still hope that I won't lose Cameron after all.

"*Had* feelings," Janey corrects me. "Sorry, Amelia. There are no specifics about what happened between them, but it's not too hard to guess."

"June," I write on the list. "Something physical happened between Cameron and Kerri that Kerri felt guilty about but Cameron didn't." *Five weeks? They must have started the affair shortly before Rowan was born.* I think this, but I don't write it down. "What's next?" I ask.

"They met up in July at a teacher's conference in New Jersey. Looks like things got pretty hot and heavy but no actual intercourse." Janey shows me the email.

*"This enforced silence is driving me crazy. This is the summer from hell! I hate not seeing you every day across the hall from me at work and am thinking about driving to Rhode Island to see you at your parents' house. I look at your picture on my phone at least six or seven times a day. The time in New Jersey was just a tease for me. I see you over and over again, in your bikini, lying on top of me. I wish we could*

*run away together and leave our current lives behind. Kenny doesn't deserve you. I don't know why you stay with him. He's cruel and vindictive. I hate that he has hit you and that I was not there to defend and protect you. Although Amelia has my brain—I know what I <u>should</u> do—you have my heart. Why haven't you responded to me? Your silence has gone on so long, I'm beginning to think you have no feelings for me at all or that I've done something to make you angry. Amelia thinks I need a physical to figure out why I am so depressed, but I know why I am depressed. I don't need a doctor to tell me it's because you are not here with me and you have stopped communicating with me. I fear I will have to tell Amelia someday what happened just to get out of our marriage. I want out. Will you make love to me then? Properly, I mean, and all the way—not just like wild teenagers groping each other in the backseat of my car."*

"July: Wild, passionate groping in New Jersey," I write on the timeline.

"Hmmm. Looks like nothing much in August—just a bunch of emails from Cameron pleading with Kerri to write back or call him. Wait! Here are two from the last day in August. She reads them out loud.

*"Cameron, I needed the time to think about what happened between us and to decide if my feelings for you were real or just an escape from Kenny. I love you, I truly do, but I feel so guilty about all of it. Let's talk when we get back to work next week. —Kerri"*

. . .

*"My darling Kerri, thank you so much for writing back to me. I'm so happy that you are not angry with me. That gives me hope that there may yet be something between us. If you decide to confess to Kenny, will you please let me know before you do so I can tell Amelia at the same time? I don't want her hearing it from anyone but me. I know how to handle her so she won't freak out and do something crazy. — Cameron"*

"Janey, these are from two years ago," I say. "Maybe it was just a fling. Men do that sort of thing now and then."

"Not *good* men." Janey looks at me with concern.

"I think my father had an affair or two and he was a good man. My mother told me that this sort of thing is natural, that men need to have different sexual experiences, but it means nothing. They always come back to their wives and families because they love them. The wives are glad to have a respite now and then from the sexual demands their husbands make on them."

I am thinking about the whips and handcuffs Cameron likes to use on me, but I don't tell Janey about them.

"Anyway, let's finish this." I pick up my pen and flip the page of my notebook.

Janey looks at me like she might be changing her mind about me being crazy and keeps pressing the print button.

"September...Dinner several times, conversations in their cars behind the school, chocolate kisses left on desks. October...Uh oh! It looks like she lifted up her shirt and flashed her boobs at him in his classroom."

"Right. October: flashed boobs." I say without emotion as I write it down.

"November...Just a lot of whining about not being able

132

to spend Thanksgiving with her and her family in Rhode Island. December...Are you sure you want to know this?"

"Of course, I do." I tilt my head and look at her expectantly.

"OK. In December, he bought and gave her a very expensive diamond and sapphire bracelet."

I can't look up. I keep moving the pen as if I am writing, but tears sting my eyes. Two Christmases ago, Cameron gave me a teapot. The memory is ruined for me now, but it comes flowing back anyway as I wrap my arms around myself and rock slowly back and forth.

"I know how much you love tea," he says. I can hear his voice as if he is standing right next to me. "This one has roses on it so every morning when you make your tea, it will be like I have brought you flowers to brighten your day."

"How sweet, Cameron! Of course, I will think about you—I *do* think about you every day and miss you every minute you are not here with me," I say. "Here, open your present!" It is a new laptop. He looks a bit surprised but very, very pleased.

It is the same laptop he has used to write emails to Kerri and the one I am spying on now. The irony of that brings me back to the present. I stop rocking and pick up my pen.

"December: Buying her expensive gifts," I write.

"Oh, honey, if this is too much, let's stop. For today anyway." Janey brings me a tissue.

"No. No. It's like removing a Band-Aid. Better to just yank it off all at once. But if you need to go home or something, I understand. I can do this myself."

"Not a chance," Janey says firmly. "I am not leaving you alone with this. Let's sort it out and then you can decide what you're going to do."

"What do you mean?"

"Are you going to stay with this man or divorce him?" She looks at me as if I have a choice.

"Oh, Janey, I could never divorce him! I promised to love him for better or for worse."

"For better or for worse doesn't mean *better* for him because he can do whatever he wants to do and *worse* for you because he doesn't care a fig about your needs or feelings." She's angry with me, or maybe *for* me. I can't seem to muster up anger right now.

I'm numb. I can't even cry.

"It means staying together and being there for each other when you lose a baby, or go through financial troubles, or find out one of you has cancer," she continues to rant. "Has *he* kept that promise? I'll tell you the answer to that. No. No, he has not."

"We don't know that yet," I say. "We haven't finished going through the emails. Perhaps this is just a record of his wayward journey and it has a happy ending for us. He sees the error of his ways and returns home, like the story of the prodigal son in the Bible."

"We'll see," Janey says, sighing. She shuts off the laptop and closes it. "I think I've had about enough for today, though. It's time for me to go home and you to start dinner for your darling husband." She puts my notebook and the papers she has printed in her oversized purse. We don't leave anything here. I don't want Cameron to find it.

She's done it just in time. I try not to look guilty as Cameron comes through the front door.

"Janey, what are you doing here?" he asks, suspicious.

"Just finishing up some work. I'm leaving." She speaks to him in her usual, brusque way. "You'll get your dinner on time, though. Amelia is very good at multi-tasking." She goes out the front door. Cameron shuts it hard behind her and locks the deadbolt.

"I don't like her," he tells me. "If she wasn't your work partner, I would never let her come here. She gives me the creeps."

"She's nice," I tell him. "She gives me advice and helps me with all kinds of things—sort of like a mother."

Cameron snorts. "A wicked stepmother, perhaps." He picks up Rowan and bounces him high in the air. "And how are you, my boy?" Rowan giggles.

I ignore Cameron's snide comments and change the subject. "I've got a roast in the crockpot. It should be ready by now." I look at the clock. It's half-past six. He's normally home around four-thirty since his last class finishes at four o'clock, but he's been coming home later and later this past week.

He notices me looking at the time. "Sorry I'm a bit late. I had some paperwork to finish up today. It's the end of the term and grades are due." He puts Rowan back in his high chair.

"Oh," I say, getting out plates and utensils. "No worries. Crockpots are perfect for keeping everything warm and ready at a moment's notice. Come, sit down. I'll get you a beer."

He sits and waits for me to hand him the beer. "How was your day?" he asks, settling back in his chair. I feel him watching me as I get a glass of water and set it by my place.

"Fine," I say. "I took Rowan to the park this morning. When he went down for his nap, I did my yoga exercises. Janey came over about mid-afternoon and helped me get some of the accounting work done. Rowan played with his toys in the living room while we did that. He's content just to be near us while he does his own thing." I dish out the pot roast, potatoes, and carrots and put our plates on the table.

"Maybe that's why he's not talking much yet. He's eighteen months old. He should be talking. You're being neglectful. You should interact with him more. People might think he's stupid if he doesn't start talking more soon. That's all on you."

"He says a lot of words." Cameron's criticism stings. "To me, at least. He says Dada all the time."

Cameron's phone buzzes. He pulls it out of his pocket and looks to see who is texting him. He starts to smile, then looks up almost guiltily. "Just work stuff," he says, putting the phone away.

"Oh," I say. "Your work follows you home now?"

"Yeah. Like I said, it's the end of the term and very busy."

We don't talk for the rest of the meal. I give Rowan his bath and put him to bed. Cameron and I watch a bit of TV. He has a few more beers and then we shut off the lights and go to bed ourselves.

It's the middle of the night, and Cameron is snoring softly. I tiptoe around the bed to the nightstand on his side and pick up his phone. It's bio-locked. I don't dare put his finger on it, and his eyes are shut. I have to know, though. I have to know who has been texting him. I think for a minute. There is a way to unlock the phone with a six-digit number passkey. What numbers would he have chosen? I try my birthday. *No.* I try Rowan's birthday. *Still locked.* I try Cameron's birthday. It makes sense that he would use his own. *Everything revolves around him.* I push that thought back. It is unkind and not what a good wife should be thinking. I type in the month, date, and last two numbers of his birth year and the phone comes to life. I slip it into the pocket of my nightgown to hide the glow of the screen. I move quickly into the bathroom and quietly shut the door. The latch as the door closes sounds loud to me. I hold my breath and listen. I can still hear Cameron snoring. So far, so good.

I press the icon for messages and see that he does have some from work. There are also messages from the credit card company, the post office, and Kerri. I open the one from Kerri.

*"I'm looking forward to the special surprise you're planning for me,"* reads the latest one from Kerri, the one that arrived during dinner tonight. *"And just maybe I'll have a surprise for you as well underneath my coat. Can you imagine what that might be? I'll give you a hint: it's nude in color. LOL. Anyway, I love that you've given me a card to open every day during Spring break. Let's meet tomorrow for dinner—tell Amelia there's a concert or something—so we can make love at least once more before I am forced to be without you for two weeks!"*

I close the app, shut off the bathroom light, and carefully put the phone back exactly where it was on Cameron's nightstand. As I crawl back under the covers in the pitch black of the bedroom, I feel Cameron's eyes on me, staring at me. I roll over to face him, planning to explain that I had a stomach ache, but his eyes are shut, so I say nothing. Did I just imagine him watching me? Yes, of course I did. If he knew I had taken his phone, he would have said something, hit me, been furious. He never ignores it when I have done something wrong. I sigh and roll over so I am no longer facing him, but as I lie awake in the stillness of the night, I can feel his hot, angry breath on the back of my neck.

# Chapter Twenty-One

"I'm spending the night at Janey's house," I tell Cameron the next morning. "She's having a party to celebrate her birthday, and it will be late. Plus, I don't want to drive home if we've been drinking. I'll wait for you to get home from work so you can watch Rowan and put him to bed. I'll feed him before I go so you don't have to worry about that."

I think my plan to keep him away from Kerri is brilliant. I have foiled his plans with some of my own.

Cameron looks up, surprised. "Why didn't you tell me before? Why wait until the last minute? I can't watch Rowan tonight. I—I have things to do."

"Cameron, I've already promised her. She is turning sixty—it's a milestone. All the girls from the office will be there. What do you have to do that you can't watch Rowan?"

"Never mind." He scowls at me. "I'll get my mother to take Rowan tonight. She'll love that. In fact, I'll take him there right now. You go do your selfish thing. Don't worry about us."

Cameron yanks Rowan out of his high chair and grabs the diaper bag. "At least my mother will not ignore him all day like you do. Go. Have fun."

I try to take Rowan from Cameron, but he turns away from me. "Cameron—wait!" He doesn't wait. He leaves the house and puts Rowan in the car. Now, I am afraid. I have made Cameron angry. I have put Rowan in danger. I am an awful mother. I am a terrible, terrible person. I watch them through the living room window as Cameron backs out of the driveway, tires screeching as he turns, then speeds down the road.

I go back to the table and put my head down on my arms. I can't stop the sobs. I'm not just crying about Rowan or Cameron. I'm also crying about my mother because I remember now—the screeching of tires, the thud as the speeding car backs up and rolls over her, the voice of my father yelling at me to "get in the car, get in the car, get in the car," and him pushing me into the driver's seat as the sound of sirens filled the night air. My mind takes me there as if it happening again, right now. I see it clearly, like I'm watching a movie.

"She didn't mean to do it," my father is telling the policemen. "She didn't see her. It's dark. It was an accident."

But it hadn't been an accident. I didn't dare tell the police the truth. I knew my father would kill me as well. But the memory is burned into my brain, like a cattle brand I can never remove. I still see every thing, hear everything, in my mind.

"I'm leaving you," my mother says, putting on her coat.

"No, you are not," my father growls back. "I forbid it."

"Just try and stop me," my mother answers. "Come with me, Amelia. It's not safe for you here."

But I am nineteen and going off to college in a few weeks. I don't want to go with her, but I follow her out the door to say good-bye. I watch her walk down the driveway from the front porch. She turns to wave at me, tears in her eyes. I do not see my father open the garage door or get into the car. I can still hear the roar of the engine, though, and the screech of tires as the brake is released and the car races out of the garage at a high speed. I hear the thud and the crunch as the car knocks her down and rolls over her. I run to my mother as she lies partially underneath the car, and kneel beside her. There is blood trickling from both of her ears onto the pavement. I touch her arm and whisper, "Mom, Mom, are you alright?" as if she is simply sleeping there. She does not answer. My father gets out of the car, pulls me away from her, and shoves me into the car before running back into the house. At least, that is how I remember it. Later, the police tell me my mother died almost instantly from head trauma and a broken spine. There are no charges brought against me, but I am sent to the psychiatric hospital for a few months to help me face up to what I have done and work through my guilt for causing my mother's death.

Janey finds me with my head still on my arms when she comes about an hour later. The tears have dried on my face, leaving streaks of dried salt. I tell her about Cameron and how my plan to keep him from Kerri has gone awry, but I do not tell her about my mother, or my guilt, or my difficulty knowing what is real and what is only in my mind. "Coping mechanism" is what the doctors in the psychiatric hospital had called it. *"You retreat into your own mind to avoid dealing with severe emotional trauma."* But, I think I am fine now. I have Janey to talk to. She helps me.

"That rat!" Janey is sympathetic. "Do you still believe

that his cheating on you is finished and he has turned over a new leaf?"

I sit quietly with my head bent. "No," I whisper. "But I can't leave him. It's too...it's too...humiliating. I still want to know everything, though."

"Let's pack an overnight bag for you, then, and you can really come to my house and spend the night. We'll work from there so there's no possibility he'll return and discover us. You told him I was turning sixty?" She smiles. "And he believed it? What a jerk. I'm only fifty-four."

When we get to her house, we do our actual jobs, our accounting work, first. She's told our boss she's not coming in today, so we really only have my work to do.

After lunch, I open the spyware program. Janey pours us both a cup of tea and hands me my notebook.

"We got all the way up to December, seventeen months ago," I tell her, reviewing my notes.

Janey scrolls through the emails until she finds the last one we read. "Okay. After that, there are a few from January through March. Cameron gave her a promise ring for Valentine's Day, which she accepted. Kerri said she feels guilty lying to her husband, Kenny. Ooh! She had a fight with her husband—not about her affair, though. She doesn't say what it was about, only that they had a huge argument and he made her sleep on the couch."

"I want to see." I lean over to read the email. Janey has moved on to the next one, though. It is Cameron's response.

*"My dear Kerri, I can't say I am sorry you had an argument with Kenny. I am hoping you are starting to see how wrong it is for you to stay with him. He treats you like dirt, not in the way you deserve. You belong with me. I treat you so much*

*better than he does! You said you never had an orgasm with him. I give those to you every time. I know you enjoy that! When was the last time he took you to dinner or gave you gifts? I want to do that—and more—every day of our lives. — AYW"*

"*Cameron, are you serious? If you are, I will talk to Kenny this weekend and tell him about us. I want a divorce so I can be with you in public—no more sneaking around.*"

"*Kerri, I want to be with you, too, but can't we continue as we are? It's worked well for us the past couple of years. Divorce is so ugly, and I really don't want to be separated from my son. You know Amelia would take him from me. There has to be another way.*"

"*Cameron, I'm so sorry, but Kenny and I had another fight. I was so angry and I wanted to hurt him, so I told him about us. Just thought you should know.*"

"*Kerri, I know you told him because he called me. It was a number I didn't recognize, so I didn't pick up. Then, a minute later, I received a call from your number, so of course, I answered it. I was very surprised it was Kenny, not you. He said, 'If you ever come near my wife again, I'll kill you. Do you understand?' I didn't know what else to say, so I just said, 'Yeah.' Kenny said, 'Good,' and hung up. Do you want me to give him an explanation and apology? I will do that for you.*"

. . .

*"No! Do not contact him! He has a terrible temper. I think it's best if we cool it for a while. I want to try and reconcile with Kenny, if possible. What you and I had was lovely and fun, but probably not realistic in the long run. I think I need space right now. Please don't call, email, or text me—I don't want to talk to you for a while. Let's just go back to being colleagues. I am releasing you from the commitment you made to me. Please remove all of the notes and photos we've exchanged from your cabinet at school. I would be so embarrassed if anyone at work finds them."*

"March: Kerri breaks up with Cameron." I write this in big, bold letters in my notebook.

"Well, that's interesting," Janey says. "Kerri seems to have more of a conscience than Cameron."

"I want to find those notes and photos," I tell her. "If he can't hide them at his work, he would have to bring them home. Where else would he put them?"

"Does he have a safety deposit box somewhere? Or a storage unit?"

"I don't think so."

"Let's look at his credit card charges. If he does, he would have to pay for it somehow."

"I don't have his passwords."

"Oh, yes, you do." Janey grins at me. "Part of this spyware thing is its ability to record every keystroke, right?"

I nod. She searches through the program until she finds what she is looking for. It looks like random letters to me, but she squints and studies it like it holds the secrets of the universe.

"I don't see anything that looks like a bank password, but there are a lot of other things here that are very odd."

"Like what?" I peer over her shoulder again, trying to see what she sees.

"He's created a fake ID card. See? This is not his school, is it?"

I see an image of an ID card with Cameron's picture, but a different name and place of employment. "Why would he do that?"

Janey scrolls down the page. "Perhaps because he is just creepy. Look. He's also created an application for college girls who want to do nude modeling in his photography studio. Does he really have a photography studio? Oh my goodness! He's set up a whole webpage with samples of his work. I don't think they are actually his photos, though. He's googled porn sites and copied and pasted some of *those* photos onto *his* webpage."

I don't know what to say. I can't make sense of any of it. Janey gets up to add more paper to the printer and I sit down in front of the computer. He doesn't have a studio, but he did tell me he wanted a camera for Christmas—a professional one—so he could take pictures of Rowan, he said.

"I want to capture every moment of his life," he told me as he wrapped his arms around me. "Don't you want that, too?"

"Of course," I said, smiling up at him. "And I love that you care so much, but we really can't afford an expensive camera right now, can we? The pictures I take with my phone are really good."

He tried to hide his annoyance. "Well, not good enough for our son. If you have something else in mind for me for Christmas, I'll just buy a camera for myself."

He did. I found it a week later in his top dresser drawer next to a box of condoms.

I don't tell Janey any of this. Instead, I write down the passwords to the porn sites I see Cameron has accessed on the internet and put them in my pocket. I don't want Janey to know I am planning to use them.

Janey comes back with two cups of tea and hands me one of them.

"So what else did you find?" she asks me.

"Not much. Just some more naked ladies he shouldn't be looking at." I get up and let Janey take the seat in front of the computer again.

"I'm so sorry, Amelia."

"It's not you who should be sorry," I tell her. "Keep going. I might as well know everything he's done."

"Well, there are no more emails through that whole summer, so I guess they really did break up for a while. They started up again in September of this year.

"Kerri, the summer apart from you was torture. I cannot do this. I still love you and want to be with you more than anything. Seeing you at work but barely speaking is painful. Please, please, please stop ignoring me. Do you feel nothing? You seem to be able to fake it in front of everyone at work, make it seem like everything is okay, but then you barely speak to me when they are gone and we are alone. I can't do that. I refuse to fake anything. I am miserable without you. — Cameron"

"Kerri, why don't you answer my emails? Amelia has never pulled at my heart strings like you do. My heart cries out for *you all the time. I would go with you in a heartbeat if you would just give the word. I would be willing to do anything —and I mean anything—for a chance to be part of your life. I miss you so much. It's so hard not knowing what you're thinking. I admit what we did was wrong, but that doesn't change the fact that you are perfect. I don't want there to be any animosity between us. My first thought has been of you every morning for over a year now. I miss our friendship more than anything else. —AYW"*

*"Cameron, I watch you when you aren't looking, and my heart breaks because I want you so much. I am very, very sorry that I got rid of all the gifts you've given me, and I wish I could get them back. I had to do that because Kenny was so jealous and I was afraid he would hurt me if I kept them. Can we start over? Can we just be friends? —Kerri"*

*"Kerri, I can't tell you how much your email meant to me. I read it over and over again a hundred times and would have kissed the screen if I dared. I wonder how we can be friends if you won't even speak to me, but of course, I would welcome that. I just know I need you in my life in any way I can get you. Can I still get you a gift for Christmas? As a friend? —Cameron"*

*"Cameron, I don't think exchanging gifts would be appropriate right now. Please, let's just keep this on a friendship level for now. —Kerri"*

. . .

*"Kerri, you were not at work today and I missed doing the little things for you, like bringing you coffee and carrying your bags. I am trying to abide by your requests but I do wonder what you feel when you see me. —Cameron"*

*"Cameron, I can't help but miss you today. Valentine's Day holds so many memories of you and being in your arms. I admit I am feeling more for you than I should. Please don't make this harder for me than it has to be. Don't leave me notes or gifts or come to my classroom. —Kerri"*

*"Kerri, I am confused by your rules—can we or can't we talk? You were cordial to me last week, but very distant this morning. You saying you miss me makes me think there is hope for our relationship. But, today, when I brought you a muffin, you rebuffed me and told me it was 'too soon for a muffin.' What does that mean? It hurts me to see you joking around with the other teachers, knowing that you don't want to do that with me. I desperately miss you and want to bring you roses, but I know that would just make you angry. I put our names and birthdates in a numerology website to see if we are romantically compatible. It said we are, but not without some work. I think we are going through that work now and it will be fine in the end. —Cameron"*

*"Cameron, as you know, I have been seeing a therapist to try and work through my feelings about you and about Kenny. I had a breakthrough yesterday and I think you'll be pleased. Can we meet tonight and talk? —Kerri"*

. . .

"Here's the last one, dated just a week ago." Janey pushes the print button with a flourish.

*"Kerri, last night was the best night of my life—getting to be with you again, touching you, kissing you, crying with you, making plans with you. I cannot tell you how overjoyed I am that you are leaving Kenny. He doesn't deserve you!"*

"So, I wonder when he is going to tell you." Janey looks at me with concern. "He doesn't say anything about leaving you, but it's obvious he wants to be with her."

I am frozen with my pen poised above the notebook. I hesitate, then write in tiny, faint letters: May/June—the end?

# Chapter Twenty-Two

I don't say anything to Cameron about what I know. Instead, I make his favorite meal and put candles on the table. Rowan has already been bathed and fed, and is happily playing with his toys in the next room. I check my hair and makeup and take off my apron. I want to look nice. I want him to want *me*. It's my fault he has wandered away. I can fix this. I did not take enough care about my appearance after Rowan was born. In fact, I don't think I've put on makeup or dressed in anything but jeans or sweatpants since I was pregnant. I've been lazy. It's no wonder he is more attracted to someone else. Kerri is not even pretty. She's very masculine-looking. If I didn't know she was married, I would think she was a butch. I'm not gorgeous, but at least I don't look like a man. If I put a little effort into our relationship, I am sure I can win him back.

"What's all this?" Cameron asks me as he comes in to the kitchen.

"I wanted to apologize for ignoring you so much since Rowan was born. I haven't been a good wife. That will change, though. I promise, Cameron. I will be whatever it is you need me to be."

His phone buzzes at that moment, and he takes it into the bathroom. I cover the food with foil to keep it warm and sit at the table to wait. The candles are burning, getting shorter and shorter. I am glad I used the long tapers.

Cameron comes back into the room and sits down. "Sorry, Amelia. I have to go back to work. I left the keyboards plugged in, and the boss is giving me a hard time. I can have dinner first, though."

He helps himself to the food and begins eating. "This is good," he says. My eyes begin to fill with happy tears as I put food on my plate. I am hopeful that this is a new beginning for us. "Almost as good as I can do," he adds. He eats so quickly I wonder how he can even taste it. Has it even been five minutes? I don't think so. He pushes back his chair and gets up. "Gotta go," he says, kissing the top of my head. "Don't wait up." He leaves, and the door slams shut behind him.

"Okay," I say into the empty air. I don't bother to finish my dinner. I put it all in the garbage.

I am not sleeping when Cameron comes home, but I pretend I am. I hear him walk over to my side of the bed. I am lying on my back and open my eyes just enough to see through my lashes, but not enough that he can tell I am awake. He is just standing there, staring at me, a pillow in his hands. He leans over, toward me, extending the pillow. I know he is going to put it over my face. I know he is going to kill me, but I don't move. I don't speak. Let him. I deserve it. I have failed as a wife. Cameron hesitates just before the pillow reaches my face and pulls back. He tries one more time before giving up. He walks around the bed and slides under the covers on his own side. *Coward*, I think. I don't want to live without Cameron. He's the only one who has ever loved me. Without him, I am nothing. But, I am glad he doesn't do it. Rowan still needs me.

In the morning, Cameron is still sleeping as I slip out of bed and get dressed. I have little to choose from since I have put all of my sweatpants and most of my jeans in a bag I will take to Goodwill today. I find a dark green pullover sweater that I haven't worn in a while and put that on. It still fits, thank goodness, and makes my hazel eyes look more green than brown today. Most of my clothes are too baggy now. I step on the scale. Well, Cameron would be pleased to see I weigh only one hundred and eight pounds. Maybe he will let me go shopping and get some new clothes.

"You're up early." Cameron's voice startles me and I step off the scale.

"I wanted to finish in the bathroom before you needed to use it. You know, put on some makeup so I look nice for you."

"I'm going to work. Why do I care how you look during the day? Did you gain weight? I saw you get off the scale pretty fast when I opened the bathroom door."

"No, not at all. In fact, I've lost about ten pounds. All my clothes are baggy on me. Would you mind if I go shopping this morning and buy something that fits?"

Cameron looks like he is about to say no, but instead, he smiles and says, "Sure, go ahead if your boss is fine with you not working today." I can't tell if he's serious or mocking me. "Just keep it under a hundred dollars."

"Okay," I say, standing on my tiptoes to give him a kiss. He turns his head away so my kiss lands on his cheek. "Um, I can still get my work done if I only spend an hour or so shopping. It's not a problem."

"Are you done in here? I've got to get ready." He's

tapping his foot impatiently and lets out a huge sigh as if I'm wasting his time.

"Yes. Of course." He's standing in the doorway, but I manage to slip around him.

I have breakfast waiting for him when he comes out of the bedroom. I am trying so hard to be a good wife and this is what good wives do, right? He sits at the table instead of running out the door like he usually does. He looks like he has something to say, so I sit down, too.

"Amelia," he says. He can't look at me. He holds his fork and bounces it up and down over his eggs. "There's something you need to know."

I say nothing. I am not going to make this easy for him. I want so badly to retreat into my own thoughts, to curl up and cover my ears, but I don't. I am stronger than I used to be, I realize with surprise. I can do this. I can listen.

Cameron clears his throat. "I am moving out for a bit. I got an apartment in the city, closer to my work. I need space to figure out what I really want." He can't look at me. He picks up his fork and then puts it down again.

"Is this about—another woman? About Kerri?" I hear my voice, but it feels like it is someone else speaking. I am finding it difficult to focus on what he is saying.

"Partially. I wouldn't cheat on you. My relationship with Kerri hasn't been physical yet, but I want to have sex with her. I need to figure it out."

I'm not surprised to hear him say this, but I think he's lying about the physical stuff. I've seen the emails. I'm not ready to give up yet, though. I can't give up. He's all I have.

"Can't you figure it out here? With me?" I try not to sound like I'm begging.

"I've tried that but it's not working. You're not what I want." Cameron finally looks at me. There is no emotion in his eyes. Not even pity. It's like he's talking to a stray dog, telling it to get out of his way.

"What do you want?" I ask.

"Everything that Kerri is."

I turn my head and stare out the kitchen window. I can hear the clock ticking in the silence that seems to drag on and on. Cameron just watches me. Finally, he clears his throat and says, "Amelia?"

I turn my head back and look at him. "Are you asking for a divorce? Your parents will be horrified," I say. I am calm. I will not cry. I want to pretend this is not real, that it is just another story in my mind.

"No, I'm not saying 'divorce' just yet. I might change my mind. And you are NOT to say anything to my parents, my brother, or any of my friends or your friends. Do you understand? Don't breathe a word of this to *anyone*." He's getting angry and his voice is getting louder. "It's none of their business."

I don't answer. Of course, I'm going to tell Janey. He can't stop me.

Cameron slaps his fist on the table, and I cringe. "Tell no one! I can read your face, Amelia."

"Okay, okay," I say. If he can lie, then so can I.

"I'll be back after work to pick up a few things." He pats me on the top of my head like I'm a dog and walks out the door.

Rowan wakes up and needs me. I don't have time to think about what just happened. I don't *want* to think about what just happened.

"Hello, baby," I coo at him. "We're going shopping today. We're going to spend lots and lots of money."

I take Rowan out of his crib, dress him, and feed him. It's only when he starts babbling nonsense words that include "dada dada" that I finally break down and cry. Rowan leaves his toys and toddles over to where I am sitting on the floor. He pats my face and puts his lips against my cheek—his version of a kiss, I think. I give him a hug and tell him that we'll be fine. Everything will be fine.

The phone rings, and I get up to answer it.

"Hello?"

"Is this Amelia?" a faintly familiar masculine voice asks.

"Yes."

"This is Kenny. You need to know that your husband is cheating on you. He and my wife are having an affair."

"What?" He's startled me. Until now, I haven't given Kerri's husband any thought.

"Yeah. They had sex several times. Kerri admitted it to me." I don't say anything so he continues, "Anyway, you need to know. He's a lying, cheating scumbag."

Kenny hangs up. He hasn't told me anything I don't know, but the phone call has shaken me anyway.

I dial Janey's number, then hang up before it rings. I can't bother her. She's working. I should be working. I pull out my files and turn on my computer.

The curser blinks at me. I blink back, then shut it off. I pick Rowan up and head out the door. It's almost ten o'clock. The stores will be open soon.

I intended to spend the morning shopping for clothes that would entice Cameron back into my arms, but instead, I find myself driving to St. Philips Church Cemetery. Rowan holds my hand as we walk slowly toward Abigail May's grave. He is fascinated by the butterflies fluttering by and the blades of grass under his feet. He stops to pick a dandelion, and I watch as he holds it to his nose. I pick a few, too. They are simple, and pretty, and free.

Rowan and I place our dandelion bouquets on the

ground in front of Abigail May's headstone. I don't want to tell her what her father has done, but I think she knows. Surely she can see everything from Heaven. "I'm sorry," I whisper.

Rowan is starting to get cranky. I have forgotten to bring any snacks or drinks for him.

"Let's go home," I say, trying to sound cheerful.

"Dada dada dada dada," he says, reaching for me.

I pick him up and carry him back to the car. "No, Rowan. I'm Mama."

He smiles and pats my cheek. "Mama," he says, for the first time.

I smile back. Today is not such a bad day after all.

# Chapter Twenty-Three

It's taken most of the summer, but I've adjusted pretty well to Cameron's absence. I mentally give myself a pat on the back. In some ways, it is easier without Cameron here. I do what I want, when I want. Rowan and I have a routine that suits us. My stomach doesn't hurt anymore and, other than crying myself to sleep each night and fighting the loneliness every day, I am doing fine. I try not to imagine all of the things Cameron and Kerri are doing together. My boss wants me to come back to the office starting next week, September 1st. I found a great daycare center that Cameron has promised to pay for, and they actually had an opening, if I am willing to start him there immediately.

"Come on, Rowan, let's get ready for school!" Rowan claps his hands and pulls his coat down from the hook in the hallway. He doesn't say "dada" much anymore, but perhaps that's because he hasn't seen Cameron in three months. That's okay with me. He says other things, like "mine" and "no" and "please," which comes out more like "peas." He'll get along just fine in daycare.

I get a sloppy kiss from him as I leave him with the teacher. I watch for a minute from the doorway. Rowan doesn't seem to mind at all that I am not there. He's busy playing with all of the new toys. The teacher plays peek-a-boo with him, and he laughs.

Everyone is fine without me.

On the drive home, I think about all the ways I could just cease to exist. I could drive into a tree. I could go to the liquor store and buy ten bottles of vodka and drink it all in one sitting. I could go for a long swim in the ocean. I could use one of Cameron's razor blades to make pretty, red designs on my wrists. I could donate both of my kidneys.

The only one that appeals to me is the vodka, so I stop and buy some. I'll keep it for a bad day. And, while I'm at it, I buy an expensive bottle of Cabernet Sauvignon that I know Cameron likes just in case he comes back. I don't know why I'm still hoping he'll come back, or even that I really want that. Habit, I guess.

I haven't been on the spyware for months. I've been too busy with Rowan and work. Janey has been far, far away. I play the scene in my head. It happened at the end of June, about two months ago, before I could tell her about Cameron leaving, but it is still fresh in my memory.

"My son is moving," Janey tells me. She sounds distraught. "I'm going to Maine for the rest of the summer to help him clean his new place and get settled in. Are you going to be all right?"

"Of course," I tell her. "You go do what you need to do."

"Thanks, Amelia. I'm so sorry I can't be there for you. Call or text me if you need anything."

"I will," I tell her, but I don't. Not once the whole summer. It's okay. I don't want to add to her burdens. She's fine without me, too. Better, actually. She doesn't need to worry about me *and* her son. She should concentrate on him. That's what real mothers do.

I can use the spyware myself. I open the program and search the keystrokes. Cameron has opened accounts with several weird dating sites. They look more like hook-up opportunity sites. He's also opened a Yahoo email account under the name Jim Swenson.

Two can play this game. I'm going to be interesting. I'm going to be someone else. I create a Yahoo email account under the name Ashely Moore and contact Jim Swenson in the adult-finder website. I want to see how far he will go.

"Hey, babe," I write. "You seem really nice. Tell me more about yourself! Love, Ashley."

I'm surprised to see that Cameron responds almost immediately. "I'm a teacher, divorced from my wife because there was no passion between us. I am a passionate lover and am looking for someone who can reciprocate that, who is willing to try new things. Can you send a picture of yourself? Here's one of me." He's attached a photo of his genital area.

I look through some magazines I have saved. There is one of a brown-haired, beautiful girl in her mid-twenties standing on the sidewalk in New York City. I take a picture of the picture and upload it to my computer. Then, I lift my shirt and take a photo of my breasts, and upload that, as well.

"Jim, thank you for responding," I write back. "I loved your picture. You certainly have what it takes to keep me happy. Are you a boob man? I hope so, because mine are large and waiting for your touch." I attach the photos I have uploaded.

I don't hear back until later that afternoon. "I wasn't

sure you are real," Cameron writes. "The photo of you on the street looks like a professional photo."

"Of course, it is," I shoot back. "I'm a model. I work out of the city mostly. I'm insulted that you doubt me. Why don't we meet in person so you can see for yourself?"

"I would like that," Cameron writes. "I'll be in the city for a conference next month. Shall we meet then? I'll send you the name of my hotel and the details when I know them."

"I would like that," I write. "In the meantime, tell me about your family, your interests, or anything! I want to know all about you!"

"I'm divorced, single at the moment, no kids, and good in bed. I'm well-off financially and would love to take you to all the exotic places you've dreamed of..."

This is unbelievable. He's such a good liar! So smooth. This is a different man than the Cameron I know. Am I sure it is really him? I check the keystrokes on the spyware app. Yep. He's typing it.

I make up stories about having a family out west and tell him how I got into modeling and about the photo shoots I've done. I throw in lots of suggestive comments and do more than just hint that I'd like him to make love to me in many ways. I am explicit. I am vulgar. I am open to his suggestions, which he gladly gives in great detail.

Over the next few weeks, I create another Yahoo email account under the name Francine Smith, attach a copy of a sexy photo of a blonde model I've found in another magazine, and send an email to Jim Swenson. I make Francine a school teacher from New Jersey looking for a job. She sends pictures of her ass and boobs, and responds to "Jim" with descriptions of things she would like to do with him that are worthy of a prize-winning porn novel. He responds in kind. How does he not recognize my body? He doesn't, though.

In the meantime, Cameron's emails to Kerri continue.

*"Dearest Kerri, now that you have left Kenny and I have left Amelia, should we think about moving in together? I want to be with you. —Cameron"*

*"Cameron, I think it's best if we don't live together right now. I need time to find myself and forgive myself for what I have done to Kenny. Perhaps we should take a break? I'm going to my parents' house in Rhode Island for Christmas. Please give me those weeks to figure out what I really want. —Kerri"*

*"My dearest, dearest love, I don't know if I can survive without you. I think about you every minute of every day. But, As You Wish. I will give you the time you need and pray that you will decide you love me as much as I love you. The celibacy will kill me! But I know it will be worth it in the end, when you come back to me and we are in each other's arms once again. —AYW"*

There are no more emails between Cameron and Kerri after this one. I check every day after work before I continue my correspondence with "Jim" as Ashley and Francine. The emails are getting steamier and even more lewd. Cameron sends them both pictures of his penis and videos of what he is doing with it. He is careful not to include his face, but I don't need a face to know it is him. This penis has a mole in the same place Cameron's penis has a mole. He's such an idiot.

There is a knock at the door. It's after eight, and Rowan is asleep. I hurry to answer it before whoever is out there rings the doorbell and wakes him up.

"Cameron!" I look through the peephole and am startled to see him standing there. "Just a second. I have to throw on a robe." What I really have to do is shut down my laptop. I hurry back to it, close all of the windows on the screen, power it down, and shove it under the couch. I am already in my pajamas and robe, so it doesn't take long to go back to the front door and open it.

"What are you doing here?" I ask. I want him here, of course. At least, I think I do. My heart says so, but my head is telling me something completely different.

"I've decided to move back in," he says, reaching for me.

I step back. "Why?" I can smell the beer on his breath.

"Why?" He looks a bit shocked. "I've missed you. I've been so lonely without you."

"Really?" I am still blocking the doorway. I can't seem to move.

"Of course. You are my one true love. How can you doubt that?"

"What about Kerri?" *And Ashley, and Francine, and the other women you are talking to online.*

"That's over, my love. It was never really serious anyway. Just a temporary fling."

I don't answer. Cameron pushes past me and puts his suitcase in the bedroom.

"Is Rowan asleep already?" He seems annoyed that I haven't kept Rowan up to welcome him home.

"Yes. Please don't wake him up."

"Well, more time for me and you then." Cameron puts his arms around me and tries to kiss me.

"No, Cameron. I—"

"I'm still your husband, Amelia. I love you. Let me show you that." He doesn't let go of me.

I am confused. He sounds so sincere. Maybe we *can* fix this. No. No, we can't. I shouldn't. Should I?

"Well, you left me and..." My voice trails off. I cannot tell him what I know about Kerri, or Ashley, or Francine, or the fake ID, or the invitations to college girls for nude photo shoots, or the porn he has been watching every day. *Or how you are beginning to hate him,* the voice in my head whispers before I can stop it.

"Kerri was a mistake. An awful mistake. I'm back now. I want to be with you." He pulls me closer to him. "Let's go to bed, Amelia. Make up for lost time." This time, I do not have the energy to resist his kiss. He takes that as agreement and pulls me behind him into the bedroom.

"I have to pee first," I tell him.

He sighs and lets go of my hand. "Hurry up."

I wonder if I can escape out the bathroom window, but it is too small and painted shut. Besides, I could never leave Rowan behind. I will have to do this. I hear my mother's voice inside my head. *"You cannot deny your husband, Amelia. Your husband will have needs, Amelia. You must always do your best to satisfy those needs. He has every right to expect that from you, Amelia, no matter how he treats you."*

I can do this. As long as he is still my husband, I have to do this. My mother said so. I shut off the part of my brain that is screaming at me about how wrong this all is and get into bed. I shut my eyes and will myself to remember nothing of what is happening, to forget the weight of him on top of me, to blot out the sounds he is making. I lie as still as I can until it is over. Cameron is gently snoring within minutes. I stare at the ceiling until I am sure Cameron is asleep, then go to the bathroom and turn on the shower. I scrub myself clean, put on a fresh pair of pajamas, and take a blanket and pillow with me to Rowan's room. I lay on the floor, curled up like a kitten, and fall into oblivion.

# Chapter Twenty-Four

"*Hi Amelia.*" I've been ignoring Janey's voicemail for almost a full week. "*Let's get together this Saturday, okay? I'll be back in town, and I miss our talks.*"

If she missed our talks so much, why did she move away? She was just supposed to be gone for the summer. "I really like it here," she told me. "I'm going to stay." And she did. She retired, and bought a house. She found another church to go to and made other friends there. She left me behind.

Everyone leaves me. I don't blame them, I guess. People tire of me. I am boring. Cameron reminds me of that often. Eric and Lyla don't come over anymore and when Cameron and I go out with them, they have a good time dancing and laughing while I just watch. Cameron says I don't need friends. He thinks me a recluse and calls me his "little hermit." He's wrong, though. I would like friends. I just don't know how to make them, or keep them, apparently.

I dial Janey's number. I can't put this off any longer. Today is Saturday. "Hi, Janey. It's Amelia."

"Amelia! I've missed you! Are you available to get together today? I've made reservations at the spa for us, hoping you can come. Our appointment is at ten. Will Lorna watch Rowan for you? I thought we could do the spa, then go out for lunch and shopping—spend the whole day together."

"Sure," I say. "I'll meet you at the spa at ten."

"Wonderful!" she says. I want to believe her.

We have a massage, a manicure, *and* a pedicure. Cameron will be angry that I have spent so much money, and there will be repercussions, but I don't want to think about that right now. I'm having a good time with Janey.

"I'm so sorry we haven't been able to get together as often," Janey tells me as we are drying our nails. "My son was diagnosed with cancer, and I needed to be there with him when he went through chemo and radiation."

Now, I feel guilty. "I'm so sorry, Janey. Why didn't you tell me?"

"I didn't tell anyone. It felt like if I didn't say anything, it wouldn't be real, you know? I didn't want it to be real. But, now that his treatments are over and he is in remission, I don't mind talking about it."

"He's doing better, then?" I feel like an awful person. I should have called her. I should have been there for her, like she was there for me.

"Oh, yes. The doctors think they caught it early enough to wipe it out completely. He should live a long and healthy life from here on out."

"That's good, Janey. I'm happy for you."

"I don't want to be far away from him, though, even now. You understand, don't you? Life is precious and life is short. I want to spend as much time with him as I can.

That's why I can't stay here and visit with you as long as I'd like. I've got to go back tomorrow."

"Of course. I understand." I wish someone felt that way about me, but I don't say that part out loud.

"We can still call and get together a few times a year."

"Of course, we can," I reassure her.

"Who knows, maybe you'll move out to Maine one of these days, and have a house next door to ours. Wouldn't that be lovely?"

"Lovely," I say, and realize that I really mean it.

We finish up at the spa and head to our favorite restaurant for lunch. After we order, Janey looks at me expectantly.

"So, have there been any more emails? Or other developments?"

"Cameron moved out."

Janey reaches across the table and grabs my hand. "Oh, I'm so sorry. No. No, I take that back. Good riddance."

"He moved back in last month."

Janey looks like she's about to swear, but she restrains herself and takes a drink instead. "Fill me in," she says.

I tell her everything. The words flow out of me like a dam bursting. I tell her about the emails, about Cameron having online affairs with the women I have been pretending to be at the same time he is proclaiming his chaste and undying love for Kerri. I tell her about the nude photo shoots and the fake ID and fake photography studio with its stolen nude photographs. I tell her how he almost smothered me with a pillow in order to be free of me.

"You can close your mouth, now," I tease her as I finish the stories.

"Oh my goodness! This is unbelievable. You should write a book."

"Maybe I will someday," I laugh.

"The man is sick." She looks serious. "Mentally ill. You have to get out of that situation. I mean it."

"Cameron is not sick." I am shocked at the thought. "He's just—he's just a man. Men have needs—"

"Absolutely not!" Janey interrupts me. Her forehead is wrinkled, and her lips are pursed and frowning. "I don't think you're safe at home, Amelia. Not with that man. You must come stay with me. Right away."

I laugh, forcing my own suspicions about Cameron back into the furthest corner of my mind. "He's not crazy or dangerous. He didn't kill me. He might have wanted to for a brief moment, but he didn't follow through on it. Everyone has those thoughts now and then. It doesn't mean a person is crazy. Anyway, he's home now, and I'm hoping he'll forget all about Kerri and we'll get back to normal soon."

"Not everyone has those thoughts, Amelia. Listen, sweetie." She takes both my hands in hers and stares at me intently. "Cameron doesn't love you. If he did, he wouldn't treat you this way."

I pull my hands out of hers. "Yes, he does. He says he does."

"So, no new emails to Kerri lately then?"

"I don't know," I admit. "I haven't looked."

"I have my laptop with me." She pushes her plate aside, pulls the computer out of her bag, and puts it on the table. "Let's see what he's been up to." I can see that she has installed the spyware app on her laptop. "Type in your account name and password." She turns the laptop around so I can do that. When I finish, I turn it back around and cross my arms.

"I don't think you'll find anything. He comes home on time every night and hasn't taken his phone into the bathroom with him at all. I never hear it buzz with messages or anything."

"Okay, let's see." Janey does a quick search. She laughs when she sees my Francine and Ashley messages to Jim. "Do you really talk to him like that?"

"I don't, but Ashley and Francine do. He would be shocked if he knew it was me."

"Oh, no."

"What?"

"I'm sorry, sweetie, but there are multiple emails between Kerri and Cameron here since January."

"Let me see!" No. No way. I had been so sure the affair was over.

She turns the computer around so the emails are visible to me. I want to slam it shut, but I can't. I read instead.

*"Kerri, I told you early in our relationship that I didn't want an affair or fling. I wanted—and still want—something permanent with you. I am willing to risk everything to find a way to do that. —Cameron"*

*"Cameron, I cry myself to sleep every night because I am so conflicted. I do love you, but I love Kenny, too. I'm so sorry, but you will have to learn to live without me. —Kerri"*

*"Kerri, if you had shown any inkling of wanting to be with me in the same way I want to be with you, I would have gladly taken you out of the whole situation and made a new life with you. I am ready and willing to risk everything. —Cameron*

. . .

*"Cameron, you have to forget me. You are nothing to me anymore. Kenny has agreed to try to save our marriage."*

*"Kerri, I feel so abandoned. I am glad that you got your husband's attention by using me, but I'm sorry I hurt so many people along the way. I am having trouble moving on even though you seem to be able to do so. I am going to move home again and try to be a good husband, but I cannot choose Amelia like you seem to have chosen Kenny over me. Even when I lie in bed with Amelia, I will be thinking about you. I doubt I will ever be happy again without you in my life, but will do as you wish. Goodbye. —Cameron"*

"She broke up with him. That's why he moved back home," Janey points out.

"Yes, but he says he's going to try to be a good husband and he has been trying. If he's trying, I should try, too."

Janey sighs. "Just keep an eye on the emails, Amelia. That way, you'll know if he slips up."

I smile as if there is nothing to worry about and close the laptop. "I will."

When I get home, Cameron is watching television. Rowan is asleep on his lap. I pick him up and carry him into his bedroom and lay him gently in his crib. I tiptoe back out to the living room and sit beside Cameron.

"Thanks for letting me have a day out with Janey," I say. I am truly grateful. It's not easy watching a two-year-old.

"No problem," he says without looking up. "Can you get me a beer?"

"Sure," I say, jumping to my feet. It's the least I can do for him since he has sacrificed his time today for me...right?

"Cameron," I ask tentatively as I hand him the beer, "are things really over between you and Kerri?"

He glances up at me. "Yeah. Why? Has Janey put ideas into your head again? That woman is nuts."

"No, not exactly," I say. "We were talking about trust, though. She thought you might lie to me—" He looks like he might throw the beer across the room, so I hurry to finish my thought. "I said you would never do that, of course, because even one little lie would destroy any possibility of trust between us."

"Correct." He's not looking at me. "I would never lie to you. I am really trying to repair our relationship, Amelia, in case you haven't noticed. I have had absolutely no contact with Kerri. Of course, I can't promise it won't happen again, but I don't mean for it to happen again or want it to happen again. I'm doing everything possible to make you under-stand that I am doing the best I can. I did like Kerri—very much—and that part of me has to heal before I can concentrate fully on us."

I am feeling bold, so I say, "There are a few things that would help me feel better about our relationship."

"Yeah?"

He doesn't seem very interested, but I tell him anyway. "I would like you to find another job, so you don't see her every day. I don't want you to be friends with her. I would also like you to tell me the truth about everything that went on between you."

"Geez, Amelia." He shakes his head in disgust. "It feels like you want to put a sword hanging over my head, ready to cut me down at any time, even if I make the tiniest little mistake. I'm not friends with Kerri. We don't have personal conversations. I can't treat her differently than I would any of the other staff members at the school. How else can I say it? You're being unreasonable."

"So, you still want a relationship with me? To stay married to me? You love me?"

"Why else would I have come back? Of course I love you. You're completely crazy, Amelia. Just stop bugging me about this."

"Janey said that men often look at porn sites." I am fudging a little. She never said that, but she *might* have, if we had discussed it. "When they are not happy at home, I mean. Is that true? Have you ever looked at porn sites?"

"Oh my god, Amelia. This is what you two talk about? That's disgusting. I would never look at porn sites."

"Never?"

"Never." He switches the channel to a football game in progress just as one of the teams scores a touchdown. "YES!" he screams in delight. I don't like—no, I *hate*— that it has taken him only three seconds to forget I am even there, but I bury the emotion, like my mother has taught me. Like a good wife should.

# Chapter Twenty-Five

It has been more difficult for me to check on what Cameron is doing with the spyware over the past three months because he is usually home before I am. On Saturday mornings, though, he runs errands and goes to the car wash, so that is the only time I have—if Rowan cooperates. Today, I am lucky. Rowan is still sleeping when Cameron leaves the house. I watch him drive away and then pull out my laptop and open the spyware application.

My heart sinks. He has accessed multiple porn sites every day at work. There is no correspondence with me as Francine and Ashley, though. I think he is afraid it is law enforcement trying to set him up since both girls told him they were eighteen, but often spoke as if they were younger. I had fun with that. Ashley and Cameron did arrange to meet, but I chickened out at the last minute and sent him a note to say that I had been called away for a modeling gig. I think that's when he started to get suspicious. Oh well. I got the information I needed. He not only cheated on me, he cheated on Kerri. I smile, pleased with myself.

I scroll down and see there are very recent emails between them, though. I am no longer smiling.

Oh, this is new. Cameron has accessed Kerri's email account. There is a message from her to her husband, dated one month ago.

*"Kenny, I hope you got my phone message. You aren't doing anything wrong. It just feels like so many things I do bother you and I think it's related to what we talked about last week. Really, I just don't know how to solve it. I'm still terribly sorry for what I did. I'd hoped that adding a puppy into our life would help. I am trying to learn more about myself so that I won't react to triggers and I will be able to see myself honestly. I'm still working on those things. I know I'm an overly sensitive girl and I wish I could change that about myself, but I still can't help feeling what I'm feeling. Whether you intend for them to or not, your words and tone sometimes hurt and pull at me, and I reflexively react. Being sick isn't helping—nor is lack of sleep. I was glad that you left me alone this morning but I was being honest when I said I wasn't mad at you, even though I would wish for you to be more understanding. I know why you snapped at me in the middle of the night about the socks and why you were irritated by my nose blowing. Kenny, I love you, and I'm tired of this unrest and upset and irritation just as much as you. I'm trying to do the best I can—I think we're both trying as much as we can. I don't know what else to say. I'm sorry I left with things so unsettled this morning. I'm half scared to send this to you lest it, or part of it, upsets you further, but I tried to say what I'm really feeling the best that I could. I hope you get this. I love you. —Kerri"*

. . .

*"Dear Kerri, I love you and I know that I've been sensitive lately. Let's just enjoy each other and not sweat the small stuff! I don't mean to attack you when I try to talk to you but I also know that I can be long-winded and repeat myself. When I go on like that it is more about me. Please just give me some room to express myself and I promise that I will not get all worked up. I can't wait to see you tonight. I love you very much. —Kenny"*

Cameron has opened and read those two emails about six times, I see. I notice he ordered silver and blue topaz earrings the same day—which happened to be my birthday —that were delivered to him at work a week later. He did not give them to me. He didn't even acknowledge my birthday this year. I think he forgot. I keep reading.

*"Kerri, I love that we are talking and flirting at work again and that you are wearing the earrings. That makes me so happy, but I want more! You are such a tease, making changes to my bulletin board, sitting at my desk and using my computer, staying after school to chat, and—especially— the way you gaze in to my eyes without speaking. When you came into my room today and held my hand, I had to hold myself back from taking you right then and there. It was the first time you have touched me in months. And even though I loved your touch, I loved your smile even more. I never want to live without it. I have no idea what is going on in your life right now, but I want so badly to tell you that I love you and want to care for you forever. We were meant to be together. When will you realize that, divorce Kenny, and be with me? I can't bring myself to say 'I love you' to Amelia any more. It*

is not possible to love two people at the same time and I choose you. —Cameron"

"Cameron, thank you for the earrings. I keep them at work, since you know I don't dare let Kenny see them. Things are complicated."

"Kerri, if we are both miserable when we are not together, we need to figure it out even if it's complicated. I don't know if it's worse to have none of you or just some of you. Why don't we just admit we want to be together and accept it? I feel like you are playing a game with me because you won't talk to me about what's going on in your life. —Cameron"

"Cameron, I want to kiss you all the time. I had a fantasy of being with you, in the most intimate way possible. I want to crawl inside your jacket and kiss you all the time but I am conflicted. Let's just continue to be best friends for now. —Kerri"

"Kerri, we are not best friends since we can't do many of the things friends do. We can't go out in public together. We can't call each other. I wonder how you can love me and stay married to Kenny for the rest of your life. I am not conflicted and if you are, it makes me wonder if you ever loved me. —Cameron"

.  .  .

There was a week after that without emails. I wonder if he's deleted them, or if they don't exist. The next one is from Cameron to Kerri again.

*"Kerri, I hate when you are sad. All I want to do is make your heart sing, not make you sad, so I wrote a poem for you. I hope you don't think it's too cheesy! Here it is:*

> *What if I said, "I want to write you a song,*
> *One that will say how I feel.*
> *How is it that*
> *You don't know by now*
> *Will this show you that my love is real?*
> *What if I said, "I want to write you a song,*
> *A song you can sing when you're blue."*
> *If the melody's fair*
> *And it's in the right key*
> *Will it show you that my love is true?*
> *The song won't climb to the top of the charts*
> *No one will hear it but you,*
> *But I know I just have to show you somehow*
> *My one needs your one to be two.*

*You must know by now that I cannot live without you. Please leave that dirtbag husband of yours and come to me. All my love —Cameron"*

I shut the computer off and go into Rowan's bedroom. He has climbed out of his crib and is happily playing on the floor with his toys.

"Come on, little man," I say, picking him up. "Let's get you washed and dressed and ready for a fun, fun day with Mommy."

He squirms, but lets me change him without too much fuss. I blow raspberries on his naked stomach, and he squeals in delight as I pull a shirt over his head.

"What's all this noise?" Cameron is home. He holds out his arms to Rowan. "Come to Daddy!"

Rowan looks at me as if he doesn't want to go to Daddy, but he has no choice. Cameron takes him from me, and they leave the room. I hear Rowan start to whimper.

"Knock it off, Rowan." Cameron is irritated. "I don't want you growing up to be a mama's boy. You can be without her for two seconds, for god's sake."

He puts Rowan in the high chair. "He's just hungry, Cameron," I say as I pull down a box of cereal and sprinkle some on the tray. Rowan smiles and shoves a fistful of cereal into his mouth.

"Cereal?" Cameron wrinkles his nose. "I hope that's not what you plan to serve me this morning."

"What do you want?"

"Eggs, sausage, hash browns, and toast."

"Okay," I say, getting out several pans. "It should be ready in about twenty minutes."

"You knew when I would be back from my errands, Amelia. It's the same every week. I can't believe you didn't have breakfast ready for me." Cameron is always a little grumpy when he's hungry. I should have remembered that and had it ready. He's right. I try to speed up as much as I can. The eggs and sausage are easy. It's the hash browns that take the most time. Cameron likes them freshly cut and seasoned. Fortunately, I have some in the freezer, ready to thaw and heat up.

"We're going to my parents' house for the day," Cameron informs me. "They haven't seen Rowan in a while."

"Oh. Okay," I say, running my fingers through my hair. I've showered, but that's about all I've done this morning. I still need to do my makeup and dry my hair and put on clothes that his mother would approve of. "When did you want to leave?"

"As soon as you're ready," Cameron says with a sneer. "Try not to take too long."

I put Cameron's breakfast in front of him, dump some more cereal on Rowan's tray, and head for the bathroom. There's no time for me to eat. I don't need to, anyway. I could stand to lose a few pounds. I can still pinch a quarter of an inch around my middle.

# Chapter Twenty-Six

We've actually had a nice time at Lorna's and Laurence's house today. They dote over Rowan, and he loves playing with the new toys they have for him. We're on our way home now. Rowan is sleepy, but not giving in, which is just fine with me. He'll go down easy when we get home.

Cameron pulls into a gas station about a block from our house. He comes back to the car with a case of beer and a bouquet of roses. He hands me the roses and leans over to kiss me.

"I love you," Cameron tells me. "I'm sorry if I've been grumpy lately. Work has been awful."

"I love you, too," I tell him, tears welling up in my eyes. I believe him. He hasn't left us again. He's sticking around. He must love me.

After Rowan is asleep, Cameron pulls me into the bedroom. "Get naked and lie on the bed," he tells me. I obey. It's been a while since he's shown me he loves me, and I look forward to being intimate with him.

I am naked, but he is not. He pulls one of the roses from the vase and draws it slowly across my stomach and thighs. He kisses me on the mouth, then neck, and on down until I moan with pleasure. He stops to take apart the petals, laying them around my nipples and thighs. He won't let me touch him. When I try, he ties my hands to the bedposts. He continues to explore my body until I think I can't stand it anymore. Only then does he remove his clothes and press his body on top of mine, entering me. It feels good, and I forget to count. He loves me, and that is all that matters.

In the morning, I am still glowing. I plan to get up before Cameron and serve him breakfast in my best outfit, my make up and hair perfect. My alarm goes off at 5:00 a.m. and I quickly shut it off so it doesn't wake Cameron. I roll over. Cameron is not beside me. I see the light on in the bathroom. It's early for him to be up on a Sunday. Could he be sick? I peek through the door, ready to fetch Pepto Bismol or Tylenol or anything he might need. I see him typing an email on his phone. I crawl back into bed and pull the covers over my head. It's the first time I suspect I might actually hate him.

I wake up again two hours later. Cameron is back in bed. I don't try to be quiet. I get up, get ready for the day, and make breakfast. Cameron comes into the kitchen, wraps his arms around me from behind, and kisses my neck.

"Last night was wonderful," he says.

"Yes," I say, putting the dish of pancakes on the table.

"These look delicious." He puts two on his plate and pours syrup over them. "Did you want to spend the day with Janey? I would be happy to watch Rowan today if you do."

That takes me aback for a minute. Then, I wonder what he will actually be doing.

"Janey doesn't live here anymore. She's too far away to visit in one day. I thought you and I could spend the day together." I can see that he is trying to suppress some frustration at my comment.

"You should drive out to see her wherever she is and stay at her place for a few days, or a few weeks—whatever you want. You have vacation time, right? Take Rowan with you. I'm sure Janey would like to see him, as well."

"I'm sure." I take a sip of coffee. I *would* like to see Janey, but I'm not letting him off the hook.

Cameron takes a bite of his pancake and chews slowly. I see him struggling to figure out how he can turn this so he gets what he wants.

"What do you want to do?" He tries to be nonchalant, but I see through him. He wants me out of the way.

"I don't know," I say. "Shall we go for a hike? We haven't done that in a while."

He looks at me like I'm crazy. "Rowan is too young to hike. He just learned to walk a year ago."

"Well, what do *you* want to do?"

Cameron takes another bite so he doesn't have to answer me right away.

"You are frustrating me, Amelia. Why would you do that? We had a wonderful night and I'm trying to do something nice for you by letting you go see your friend, and you totally turn this around. Do whatever you want. I don't care." He gets up and grabs his jacket. "I can't deal with your nonsense. I'm going out."

I shrug. I really don't care anymore. I take our dishes to the sink. He goes out and slams the door behind him. He's left his phone on the table, and it buzzes. I pick it up. There is a text from Kerri glaring at me. Cameron comes storming

Cheryl Thomas

back into the house and sees me with his phone in my hand. He grabs it.

"Stop being so nosey," he snaps at me, glancing at the screen. It is blank. I can tell by his expression that he is not sure if I've seen anything or not.

"It buzzed, and I thought it was mine," I say. "I only realized it wasn't when it didn't recognize my face."

He grunts, satisfied that he's gotten away with it again. "It was probably Eric. He wanted to meet up with me today. I'm going to his place to hang out for a while and work on some music. I don't know when I'll be home." He puts the phone in his pocket and leaves the house again. This time he doesn't slam the door.

I get Rowan up and dressed, then give him toys to play with in the living room while I turn on my laptop. I want to see what he was doing at five o'clock this morning. There are multiple emails back and forth.

*"Kerri, I want to be with you, but I am not sure you feel the same way. I want to bring you roses and draw one gently across your skin, to feel you sigh and moan gently underneath me. I know it won't do any good to try and persuade you to leave Kenny. You need to make that decision on your own, but that is what I would like you to do.—Cameron"*

*"Cameron, the thought of leaving Kenny for you scares me. What if you tire of me or change your mind?"*

*"Kerri, I made up my mind a long time ago that being with you is worth anything I have to go through. I was very*

jealous when you got flowers from Kenny at work this week. I was hurt when you left work on Friday without saying goodbye. It made me feel like you thought I acted like an idiot this week. I couldn't get you out of my mind last night. I know I can make you happy. You just have to be willing to give me a chance. —Cameron."

"Cameron, my heart and my head are telling me two different things. I'm conflicted. Perhaps you should meet someone else who will treat you better. I can't hurt Kenny again."

"Kerri, Your comments make me feel that you love Kenny more than me. All I want is to embrace you and tell you that we belong together. I've waited all my life for you. We are meant to be together. Why are you fighting this? I feel like I am in limbo—knowing what I want, but waiting for you to decide what you want. I haven't told Amelia I love her in over a year but I tell you that every night because it's true and I want to assure you of that. Continuing to pretend there is nothing between us will not work, nor will trying to forget each other. We need to be together. Let's meet tomorrow behind Grandma's Restaurant so we can talk about this. — Cameron."

"Okay. I do miss you. Kenny will be at church in the morning, so I should be able to get away and meet you there at 10:00. I'll leave him a note saying I went shopping. — Kerri"

. . .

Nice. Perhaps I'll take a drive to Grandma's Restaurant. Or perhaps I'll think of a better way to get even.

# Chapter Twenty-Seven

I pack a suitcase and put Rowan in the car. I've decided to visit Janey after all, but before I go, I purchase a nanny-cam from Best Buy with cash and install it in our bedroom. It's a small teddy bear and looks very cute sitting on top of my dresser with my other knick-knacks, facing the bed. If Cameron brings Kerri here, I want to know. In fact, I will probably post the video on Facebook. Maybe I'll put it on Cameron's fake photography studio page. Or both. I could also send it to his mother. So many choices.

I leave Cameron a note thanking him for his wonderful idea about me visiting Janey, saying that I've thought about it, and am taking him up on his suggestion. I call my boss to tell him where I'm going and working remotely is no problem. He loves Janey. "Stay as long as you like," he told me.

I do not leave Cameron prepared meals. I do not wash the dishes. I do not even pick up Rowan's toys. Perhaps Kerri will trip over them when she comes. I imagine her lying on the floor, head cracked open, bleeding out on my living room carpet, and feel nothing but satisfaction.

Cameron will call an ambulance. The medics will save her. She will be fine. But, it will be a warning. She should not come to my house. She should not touch my husband.

I stay at a hotel that night only a few hours away from Janey's house so I can finish the drive in the morning and have a full day with her. It would be rude to arrive in the middle of the night, anyway, no matter how anxious I am to see her.

Janey is delighted to see me. There is a high chair for Rowan in the kitchen and a crib set up in the guest room. "Just in case you ever were able to come," she tells me. "How are you? What has been going on? Tell me everything!"

"Things are going well. At least, Cameron moved back home and has been very attentive to me and Rowan." This is mostly true.

"His affair with Kerri is over?"

"He says it is." I don't want to lie, so I'm trying to be careful with my words.

"Uh huh." Janey looks skeptical and she speaks with a hint of sarcasm. "Did he move on to someone else, or is he really repentant and madly in love with you again?"

"Oh, there's no one else. I'm absolutely sure of that," I tell her. "Ashley and Francine are finished." I can't help giggling. Janey snorts with laughter.

"Too bad he never met them in person," she says, trying unsuccessfully to stop laughing.

"Can you imagine his face? Looking for his gorgeous, sexy model and seeing me instead?" I've managed to stop laughing but I make no effort to hide my grin. "That would have been priceless!"

"Oh, my! If you'd gone through with it, I would have insisted that I be there, too...with my camera...to...document...the...whole thing." Janey is having trouble talking, she is laughing so hard.

Finally, she gives a sigh and holds her belly. "It's been a while since I've laughed so much. My stomach hurts, but it was worth it! Would you like some coffee or tea?"

"Tea, please," I say. "I've missed talking with you like this. Are you ever coming back?"

"You know I can't. I need to be here for my son. But you're welcome to move here anytime!"

I sip my hot tea and think that I might just do that someday, but I don't tell her that. We chat late into the night about everything *but* Cameron and make plans to go shopping in the morning. I have Cameron's credit card. I took it from his wallet last night, along with all of the cash he had in there. I hope he misses it.

"Would you like to look at his emails, for old times sake?" she asks me when we get back from our shopping trip the next day.

"Sure," I say. "Why not? Let me put Rowan down for his nap first." He's such a good boy. I give him his favorite blanket, and he settles down in the strange crib without a whimper. When I come back to the living room, Janey has the computer open, ready for me to log in to my spyware account.

"Oh, your husband has been busy," she says, scrolling through the emails.

"I know." I sit beside her. "Just read the ones from yesterday and anything that's there from today."

She takes her hands off the keyboard and sits back. "You know? Okay, young lady, fill me in. What's really been happening?"

"Kerri broke it off for a bit, but they still pine for each

other. They were going to meet and talk about their relationship."

"Does Cameron know you're here?"

"I left him a note. He actually suggested I visit you, so he won't be mad. I think he'll be glad, actually, because he can see Kerri all he wants to without me there."

"That doesn't upset you?"

I don't answer her right away. It takes me a minute to put my thoughts together. "It does, I guess. But lately I've been thinking that if she wants a cheater, she can have him. He cheated on me. He will cheat on her—actually has cheated on her already, if you count Francine and Ashley and all the other women he was sexting with. She's just as much a cheater as he is so I guess they deserve each other. I can only hope she will cheat on him and make him as miserable as he's made me."

"That would be sweet revenge, wouldn't it?"

Janey has a different definition of revenge than I do, but I don't tell her that. "Yes," I say instead.

"What's the last email you read?"

"The one about them meeting at Grandma's Restaurant."

Janey skims through the emails. "Okay. There are just a few more after that."

I lean over her shoulder and follow along as she reads them out loud.

*"My dearest, darling Cameron, I was afraid Kenny was going to show up at work today and catch us. Thank you for the chocolate kiss you left on my desk as well as the gift you got for my father. He will appreciate that. I've told him about*

*you. You know I can tell him anything. He said he will support any decision that I make. That's huge for me. —Kerri*

*"Kerri, I loved that you came into my room after school and did cartwheels. That's what my heart does every time I see you. I wonder how many different ways there are for me to tell you that I love you. No one has ever loved you like I do. Remember that. —Cameron*

Janey snorts and rolls her eyes.

"Keep reading," I say.

"Well, next is not an email. It's all the porn sites he accessed after writing that one to her."

"I can't believe he looks at porn at work. I hope he gets caught." I am a little surprised at my reaction. Won't that reflect badly on me? I couldn't keep his interest so he turned to other things. But, I am beginning to think that other people *should* know Cameron is not as perfect as they believe he is. The golden boy who is so talented and admired by everyone *should* lose his crown.

"He's checking Kerri's work email, too. She must have given him her password. I wonder why he does that." Janey adjusts her reading glasses and leans forward, studying the screen.

"I think he's jealous of the other men Kerri talks to—including her husband. There were emails a while back between Kerri and a guy named Joe that made it sound like Kerri may have gone out with him a few times, and maybe they kissed or something."

"Before she was married?" Janey leans back in her chair and looks at me.

"No. At the same time she and Cameron were exchanging spicy emails. Or maybe between, when she wasn't talking to Cameron. I don't know."

Janey shakes her head and scrolls down the page. "Look! He contacts someone named Swallower and asks her to send him a picture. He says he's looking for someone to have fun with.

"Disgusting," I say.

"I agree." Janey keeps reading. "Then, he contacts two more girls and tells them he's a recently separated teacher looking to meet someone to share some good times with. He claims he has never tried anything like this before. Ha! What a liar!"

"I'm starting to see that," I admit.

"Okay, here's the next email." Janey opens it.

*"Dear Kerri, I enjoyed playing footsie with you at the staff development this afternoon. It gives me hope that you are beginning to reciprocate my feelings for you. When you are tired of the abuse from Kenny, I will be waiting. He is not good for you. I feel that, in you, I have found someone I've waited a lifetime to find. I will always love you. —Cameron"*

*"Dear Cameron, I had a breakthrough in therapy, and I suspect you will like the direction it is going."*

*"Dear Kerri, I wrote another poem for you. I can't help but be a romantic when it comes to you! Let me know what you think...*

*When you enter the room*
*I feel lighter.*
*A smile comes to my face.*
*I feel relaxed, complete.*
*When you brush against me,*
*The world around me becomes a different place:*
*Richer, fuller.*
*And every nerve in my body trembles*
*When you reach out for me.*
*Purposefully*
*Telling me you want to be near me.*
*The world around me disappears*
*And I am yours alone.*


"He's not a very good poet, is he?" Janey remarks.

"No." I giggle.

"Well, I'm glad to see you can laugh about it." Janey looks at me, concerned.

"Sorry," I say. "It's like this Cameron is a different one than the Cameron that's my husband. This one is a sorry, sad-sap wimp. I don't even like him."

Janey smiles. "I'm proud of you, Amelia."

I'm startled by that. "Why?"

"You've changed, too. You're stronger. You were a little bit of a doormat with him before. Sorry to say that, but you were. And now, well, you admit that he might be wrong about things."

I am uncomfortable with her comments, so I just shrug and say, "Please keep reading."

"Well, he then contacts a Marissa, a Gaby, a Jennie, and a Michelle through Craigslist personal ads. Marissa sends him pictures. Oh my goodness! Do you want me to read you his ads?"

"Of course," I say. How bad can it be?

"If it's too much, you tell me."

"I will. I'll be fine."

"There are quite a few. All of them are from Cameron using a variety of pseudonyms." Janey begins reading.

*"Read your ad and it struck a chord with me. I have been feeling similarly for some time now Why don't you write and tell me what "fun and excitement" would mean for you? Picture would be welcome, but not essential."*

*"I've got some time on my hands and would love to be your playmate. Write me and tell me what you'd like. Maybe we can meet for lunch one day (might as well get an early start...)"*

*"I know a few spots in the mall where we can be daring. Write and tell me the most daring place you've ever had sex. I'll tell you about the time I made love on a picnic table in a public park."*

*"Saw your ad and your photo. Beautiful... Why don't you tell me more specifically what you're looking for and if I can help. I'm twenty-eight, just a little under six feet, and 183 pounds. Not an Adonis by any means, but I have been told I know how to pleasure a woman. Would love to explore the options with you..."*

.  .  .

*"Gaby, you say you're looking to give the right man a nice wet blow job, but you don't say what would make him the right man. I'm a twenty-eight-year-old Caucasian who loves to give and receive oral. Whether I'm the right man or not, I'd love it if you'd send me a shot of your face like you mentioned in the ad."*

*"My wife and I are looking to add a third person to our bedtime play, and you sound like a lot of fun."*

I almost choke on that one. "Stop," I say. "Stop reading. Let's check the nanny cam. I'm sure it will prove him innocent of actually doing anything. It's just talk, just fantasy."

Janey clicks on the camera icon and a video opens up. I watch in horror as Cameron and Kerri walk into the bedroom, kissing and groping each other. They take off their clothes and crawl under the blankets on the bed. Cameron throws them off and flips Kerri over so she is on her stomach and he enters her from the back. I start to count his thrusts, but stop myself. I reach over and close the laptop.

"I don't need to see any more. I'm not sure I can do this," I say through gritted teeth. I feel like I'm going to vomit. I start to retreat into the solitary place in my mind where no one can find me, where I don't have to think about this, but Janey's voice pulls me back.

"Do what? Stay married to a scumbag?" Her tone is stern, but her face is sympathetic.

"Yes. I know I should forgive him. I know marriage is sacred and we made a promise to be together. I know men do these kinds of things all the time and that it is most likely the wife's fault for not being attractive anymore, or boring, or too busy, but I'm not feeling good about it. I've tried everything I know to bring him back, but it's not working. What am I doing wrong, Janey? I want to love him like I should, but my thoughts—my thoughts are sometimes not good."

"Sweetie, that's perfectly normal. And where did you get the idea that it's your fault? *He's* making these decisions on his own. *He's* behaving this way."

Janey doesn't understand. She doesn't have a husband. She got pregnant and never married the man who put her in that position. She says she didn't like him much and wasn't going to be tied to him for the rest of her life. I think she is the bravest person I've ever met.

"Life is different when you're married," I tell her. "You give up your independence in exchange for protection and provision." I try to sound like I'm quoting someone wiser than we are. She's having none of it.

"That's ridiculous."

I'm starting to agree with her, but I can't admit it yet. It goes against everything I learned growing up. Everything I've been striving to be. Calm, patient, loving, loyal...

"Do you really think Cameron protects you and provides for you?" Janey asks.

"Of course."

"Really?" She gives me a hard look. "I've seen those bruises on your arms and legs. I can only imagine what the parts I can't see look like. That's not protection, Amelia."

"I—I deserve it." I haven't been a perfect wife. I've burned a few dinners, been unable to always clean the house like I should or keep Rowan's toys picked up. I've spent time spying on him. And—probably the worst thing—my thoughts have been rebellious and resentful lately.

"No, you don't." Janey interrupts me. "You deserve to be treated with respect. He's not doing that. You have to put your foot down, sweetie. Tell him to cut off all this—" She gestures to the computer. "Or you will leave him. He has to make a choice."

"I can't talk about this anymore." I'm tired. I'm confused. I want to retreat into my own world for a while, where it is quiet and no one is telling me what I should do.

"Get some rest," Janey tells me. "We'll talk again in the morning."

"Goodnight," I say. In the morning, I will not be there. When I know she is asleep, I write her a thank-you note for her hospitality and leave it on the kitchen table. Rowan is sound asleep and doesn't even stir when I pick him up and take him to the car. I turn on the engine and begin the long drive home.

It's not difficult for me to stay awake. My mind is racing. I was wrong to leave Cameron alone. What man couldn't resist the temptation without his wife there to meet his needs? I realize that now. This is my fault. He has always told me so, but I've been rebellious and cranky and did not want to admit when I was wrong. I can't throw away my marriage. I have to fix this. I have to get home before he makes another mistake he can blame me for.

I see Kerri's car in the driveway when I arrive at 7:00 a.m. She is blocking the garage door so I park on the street in front of my house. Rowan is just starting to wake up.

"Let's go see Daddy," I tell him. His diaper is soaked. I feel the heaviness of it as I pick him up.

"Wet!" he complains, tugging at it.

"Okay, I'll change you before we go in, but we have to hurry. Daddy needs us," I tell him, grabbing a diaper from the bag on the floor. He lies down obediently on the seat and I quickly put on the dry diaper and change his clothes. I see a light turn on in the kitchen.

"Are you hungry? Let's go inside and I'll make breakfast for all of us," I say.

"Eat!" Rowan crawls out of the car and tugs at my hand.

We walk up the steps and unlock the front door. I am afraid, but I take a deep breath and go inside.

"Go play with your toys while Mommy makes breakfast," I tell Rowan. He happily complies. I can hear Cameron and Kerri in the kitchen. A cabinet door shuts. Food is sizzling. Plates and silverware are being put on the table. I walk quietly to the doorway and stand there, watching them. They haven't noticed me yet. Kerri is humming and flipping pancakes as Cameron tries to figure out the coffee machine.

"Hi," I say, a little louder than I intended. "I'm back."

Both of them jump at the sound of my voice.

"Oh, hi Amelia." Kerri is the first to recover. "I stopped by to give Cameron a ride to work this morning, and he invited me to stay for breakfast first."

I know she is lying. She has been here since yesterday. I have seen them on the nanny cam. I don't answer. I just tilt my head and look at Cameron.

"You weren't here to make me breakfast, and she offered," he says. "By the way, you left the house a mess. I can't believe you did that. That is reminiscent of your crazy days, Amelia, when you were pregnant with Rowan and didn't do anything around the house to take care of me. I was worried about you."

"Kay-zee!" Rowan comes into the kitchen and tries to climb into his high chair. "Kay-zee Mommy!"

"Well, now that you have Amelia back, I should go," Kerri says to Cameron. "I'll just grab my stuff and see you at work." When I do not move out of her way, she looks to Cameron for help.

"Amelia, can you please help with the coffee at least?" Cameron takes my hand and pulls me out of the way. I see Kerri roll her eyes as she walks around me. I know she is going to get her clothes and makeup from our bedroom. How long did she think she was staying? Will she have a large suitcase or an overnight bag? I don't get to see that. Cameron is holding my wrist tightly. When we hear the front door open and shut, he finally lets go.

"What were you thinking, Amelia? Leaving like that?"

"You told me to go visit Janey, so I did."

"You said you weren't going to go. Then, I came home two days ago, and you were gone."

"I left a note—"

"That's not the point!" Cameron scowls at me. "What was I supposed to do? You put me in a bad position. Alone, here, in the house. A very messy house, I might add. Kerri came and rescued me. She cleaned up the dishes, put Rowan's toys away, made the beds—geez, just about everything *you* should have done."

*Including having sex with you*, I think, but don't dare say out loud.

The pancakes are starting to burn. I can smell them. I turn off the flame and move the pan to a cold burner.

"Eat!" Rowan bangs on his tray with two fists. "Kay-zee Mommy! Eat!"

"Get my coffee, Amelia." Cameron sits down and impatiently taps his cup on the table.

I want to scream at both of them, but I only do it inside my head. I'm frozen. I can't move.

"Now!" Cameron shouts and startles me out of my stupor. So, I do it. I get coffee for Cameron and pancakes for both of them. When they are busy eating, I go into the bedroom, remove the sheets from the bed, take them out to the backyard, and set them on fire.

# Chapter Twenty-Eight

I am very polite and kind to Cameron after that. I make sure the house is spotless and that his clothes are clean and pressed. I get up early every day to do my hair and makeup. I wear sexy outfits and make delicious meals. I am clean and naked under our new sheets every night, ready for anything he might want. I send him off to work with a kiss and greet him with hugs and a beer when he comes home, no matter what time it is. I don't ask questions. I am the perfect wife.

It hasn't made any difference. He's already gone this morning, and I don't know where. It's the weekend. I was hoping he would take Rowan and me to the zoo for a nice family day out. He said no, that he has other things to do that were more important today—like go to the carwash and talk to Kerri, although he didn't really say that last part.

I stare at the computer screen, reading and re-reading the emails from the past week.

. . .

*"Darling, being with you when Amelia was out of town helped me make a difficult decision. I spoke about it with my therapist, and she has encouraged me to do what I need to do for me. So—I wanted you to be the first to know I have left Kenny and filed for a divorce. Even if you no longer want me, I needed to do that for myself. He has been so cruel to me. We went hiking last week and he left me alone on top of the mountain just because I told him I was having doubts. I had to find my way back down by myself and then call an Uber to get home. He's made me sleep on the couch after arguments instead of letting me have the bed. And those are just two examples! I have learned through my therapy sessions that I don't deserve to be treated like that. If I had never met you, I would not have known how kind and compassionate a man could be. —Kerri*


*"Kerri, it's 3:20 a.m. and I can't sleep, thinking about you. I hate that you still want to keep us a secret. I want to go public with our relationship. I want everyone to know I love you and you love me. I haven't even told Eric about us yet, but I think he suspects that you are the source of my joy just as Amelia is the source of my unhappiness. When do you think you will be comfortable telling your parents about us? Or our friends about us? As soon as I know you feel the same way, I will divorce Amelia and we can start our life together. —Cameron"*


*"Cameron, I just need a little more time. I have been anxious about this whole thing, especially after Amelia caught us. I am afraid of what she might do. I had to get a prescription for valium from my psychiatrist. I have the same cold that you*

*had, and people have noticed, so we may not be as secret as we thought! It's not surprising that we ended up with the same cold since I had my tongue down your throat Monday night. It is definitely worth it, though!"*

*"Cameron, according to my therapist, I am ready to take the next step. It has been hard for me to trust anyone, but I can now say I completely trust you and want to be with you in public as well as in private. I have had enough alone time and want to be in a relationship with you and have children with you."*

*"Kerri, you don't know how long I've waited for this. I want to be with you, too. Let's talk on Saturday. I'll reserve a room for us at the Hilton. I'll meet you there around 3:00 and we can spend the night there together. —Cameron"*

Saturday. Today is Saturday. I go into the bedroom and open the closet. Cameron's clothes are still there. He's not leaving me yet. There is still time.

"Do you want to go to the zoo with Mommy?" Rowan is fussy today, and I need to find something to do with him.

"Yes!" He nods vigorously and runs to the closet for his shoes. I try to help him, but he pushes me away. "I do it!"

"Okay, little man. You do it." He's getting so big. He struggles a bit and manages to get his shoes on the wrong feet, but I don't correct him. "Perfect!" I say instead. "Let's go."

He puts himself in the car seat, but I help him buckle in. He's not fighting me on that yet, thank goodness. I like that he's becoming more independent, but it takes double the time to get anything done.

I back out of the driveway and head toward the Parkway. It's the quickest way to the zoo so I take it even though it is old and narrow, and I have to drive fast to stay out of the way of aggressive drivers. Usually, I avoid this road, but today I am feeling a bit reckless.

I merge with the traffic flying by me at seventy miles per hour and try to keep up. My knuckles are white from gripping the steering wheel so tightly. I take a deep breath and try to relax. This will be fun. I think we will go see the monkeys first. Rowan will like that. He is playing with his stuffed monkey in the backseat.

I see the exit for the zoo and put my foot on the brake to slow down. Nothing happens. I press harder. The pedal drops to the floor with no resistance. I begin to panic and pump the brakes over and over again. Nothing happens. I don't know what to do. I hear a scream and realize it is me. I swerve into the exit lane. An angry car horn blasts behind me. We slow down a bit going around a curve, but I still can't stop. I hit the car in front me. The air bags explode, and now I can't see a thing. The car stops, though. We are in the ditch at the side of the road. I turn around to make sure Rowan is okay. He has dropped his stuffed monkey on the floor and is reaching for it. He starts to cry, but he doesn't look hurt. My forehead is bleeding. My legs hurt, but I think they are just bruised. I can move them.

A police officer opens my door.

"We have an ambulance on the way," he tells me.

"I'm fine," I manage to say between sobs. "But can they please check out my baby? I think he's okay, too, but I just want to be sure."

"No problem. Just sit tight," he says. His voice is

comforting. It surprises me that he is not angry with me. "What happened?"

"I tried to stop, but there's something wrong with the brakes, I think."

There are a whole bunch of policemen here now. One of them crawls under my car with a camera. I hear the ambulance sirens not too far away now. I have my eyes closed and they think I am not listening, but I am. I hear one of them say, "The brake line is either very well worn or cut with a jagged tool. It's hard to tell until we get it back to the garage. Add that to the report."

Worn. I'm sure it's just worn. It's an old car. Who would cut a brake line? Our neighborhood has never had hooligans who would do that. It's a safe place to live.

I call Cameron. He doesn't answer, so I leave a message. "I've had an accident. I'm on the Parkway exit for the zoo, but the ambulance will be here soon. I'm not sure what hospital we will be going to. I'm fine. Rowan's fine. I think they will just check us out and let us go. The police think the brake line was worn, and that's why I couldn't stop and I hit the car in front of me. Anyway, call me when you get this message. I should know which hospital by then so you can come get us. Bye."

The doctors say Rowan is fine, but I need stitches in my forehead. I refuse to let anyone take Rowan, so he sits on my lap and sucks his thumb while they put in sixteen stitches. It's near the hairline, so I think it won't make me look too bad once it's healed. I can get bangs. I've always wanted bangs anyway, like Leslie Ann Warren in Cinderella. If I could look like her, I'm sure Cameron would lose interest in Kerri and in anyone else, for that matter. Why haven't I thought of this before?

They want to do an MRI to make sure I am not

concussed, but I refuse. I just want to go home. The nurses bring the discharge papers, but Cameron still hasn't called back. I try him once more, but it goes straight to voicemail. We wait for an hour. I buy chips and water from the vending machine and give them to Rowan to tide him over. When Cameron still hasn't called back, I phone his mother.

"Of course, I'll come get you." She sounds worried. "I'll be there in fifteen minutes. Shall I bring a sandwich for Rowan?"

"That would be wonderful." I am relieved. She's a mom. Even if she doesn't approve of me much, she understands what Rowan needs.

A half hour later, we are in her car. She is driving slowly and carefully, like she thinks I'll be afraid. I'm not afraid. I just want to get home. My head hurts.

"What happened, Amelia?" She glances at my stitches with disgust.

"Something was wrong with the brakes, and the car didn't stop. I hit the car in front of me and that knocked us into the ditch."

"Well, the car is probably totaled. I don't know what you'll do now. How will you get to work?"

I haven't thought that far ahead. "I don't know," I say.

"You could have been killed. Or killed Rowan. You should have made sure the car was safe. How would you feel if Rowan died because of you?"

"Rowan is fine. Not a scratch. I'm the one who got banged up a bit." My tone is a bit nasty, but I don't care. I should care. She came and got us, after all. "I'm sorry. Thank you, Lorna, for coming to pick us up."

"Of course, dear," she says. She pulls into my driveway. "Now, take care of that grandson of mine. He's precious to all of us."

"I know, Lorna. I will." I get out of the car and unbuckle Rowan from his carseat. I can't carry him. It makes my head spin. I put him down and take his hand. "Come on, Rowan. Let's go make dinner for Daddy."

"Eat!" he yells, delighted.

Cameron is sitting on the couch, drinking a beer and watching TV.

"Where have you been?" he growls at me.

"At the hospital," I say, pointing to my head.

"That's really gross, Amelia. You should try not to be so clumsy. I've been waiting here." He's in a very bad mood.

I wonder why he is not at the Hilton with Kerri. "I was in a car accident. Your mom picked us up from the hospital since you didn't get my message."

Cameron turns down the volume on the TV. "What? You wrecked your car?"

"Yes." I can't deny it. I did wreck the car. "I'll call the insurance company in the morning."

"You can't use mine. You'll have to find another way to work."

"I was hoping Kerri could pick you up and I could take your car."

"Kerri is not going to pick me up. I don't want her to pick me up."

"Well, someone else from work, then?"

"No. You had the wreck, so you'll have to figure it out. You can't inconvenience me because of your mistakes."

I thought he would be thrilled to have an excuse to be with Kerri. Obviously, I am wrong. I wonder what has happened between them. I notice he is holding a frozen bag of peas against his stomach.

"Did you want peas with dinner?" I ask.

"Sure," he says, throwing the bag of peas at me. I can't

react fast enough. My head is still spinning. They hit my cheek and drop to the floor. I pick them up and nearly faint with the effort. I am trying to think what I had planned for dinner, but my thoughts are cloudy and muddled.

I wander into the kitchen and open the refrigerator. Good. There is a dish of lasagna just waiting for me to put in the oven. I must have prepared it before I left this morning. I can't remember.

It is three days later before my head has cleared and I start to feel like myself again. I do remember calling my boss and telling him what happened.

"Take time to heal," he told me. "Don't worry about work. I'll have a temp come in and cover for you for a couple of weeks. Just take it easy and do exactly what the doctor tells you to do."

"I will. Thanks." Lorna has taken Rowan to her house. I wanted to object, to say I was perfectly fine to watch him, but I didn't have the strength to argue with her.

Today, two police officers show up at my door at 9:00 a.m. Thank goodness I had the strength to get dressed today. It's only been three days since the accident. I let them in.

"Would you like coffee?" I ask.

"No, thank you." Officer Kendrix answers for them both. "We won't be long. We just have a couple of questions to ask you."

"Okay," I say.

"This is about your accident."

"Okay," I say again, wondering if I am in trouble. There was damage to the other car, but not as much as mine. I'm pretty sure he drove away from the accident. I don't think he was hurt. But, you never know. I wonder if they are here to arrest me for causing the accident.

"We did an investigation on the cause. You said you had no brakes, right? Your brakes gave out?"

"Yes. I tried to stop. I'm so sorry I hit that car."

"Um, yes, we know that. Is there anyone you know who would try to hurt you?"

I am shocked. "No!" I say emphatically. No one even sees me. I am the invisible woman.

"Well, um, the reason we ask is that, um, the brake line in your car was cut. Definitely cut. At first, we thought it was just worn out, in which case you would have been responsible for the accident. However, when we took a closer look, it was clear that someone had deliberately cut the brake line."

"I'm sure you must be mistaken." His suggestion that it was cut on purpose surprises me. "I don't have any enemies. I'm just an accountant. My husband is a teacher. We mind our own business. Who would want to hurt us?"

"That's what we're trying to figure out," Officer Kendrix says.

They are quietly staring at me, hoping I'll give them a clue. I really don't know what to say.

"Well, maybe some teenagers did it for a prank?" I offer my best suggestion. "Or on a dare? I've heard that happens sometimes."

"Does anyone else drive your car?"

"No. Just me, mostly, although Cameron—that's my husband—takes it sometimes when his car is low on gas or something."

"Do you have a doorbell camera or security camera anywhere on your property?"

"No."

"How about your neighbors? Do they?"

"I don't know." I'm not being helpful, but it's not on

purpose. I can see their frustration growing. I want to tell them about the fight between Kerri and Cameron, but I don't. It's too complicated. I'm wondering, though, if Kerri did this. Or maybe her husband? He sounded angry when he called me that one time. I shake off the thought. When would either of them have had access to my car? Never, unless they snuck into the garage at night when we were sleeping because my car is always parked inside the garage at night. It's not even worth bringing them up.

"Well, thank you, Mrs. Dallas. We'll check the neighborhood cameras, if any, to see if we can get more information. It's possible it happened somewhere else—a mall parking lot, at work, or just about anywhere so we may not find out anything that way anyway. In the meantime, here's my card if you think of anything else we should know." Officer Kendrix hands me his business card and shakes my hand.

"Thank you," I say politely.

I show them out, then call Cameron. I am surprised when he answers.

"Cameron, the police were just here."

"What? Why?"

"They say someone cut the brake line in my car and asked if we had any enemies."

"Cut the brake line? That's insane. I'm sure it's just worn out. Your car is old. I've told you several times that you need to get a new one, but you've always put it off."

He has? I can't remember him ever telling me to get a new car. "We can't afford a new car," I say.

"Haven't you been saving money? I thought you told me you were putting money aside?"

My head is throbbing. My paycheck automatically goes

into our joint account every week. I don't have my own account. What is he talking about?

"Amelia? Are you there?" Cameron sounds concerned.

"I...uh, I...don't remember having a savings account."

"Oh my goodness, Amelia. Don't go crazy on me now. You have a savings account. You keep the register for it in your top dresser drawer. If it's not there, I don't know what you've done with it."

"Oh, of course," I say. "Of course. I'm sure it's there. Did the police talk to you?"

"No. Not yet. What did you tell them?"

"I said we don't have any enemies and that it was probably some teenage prank or something."

"Good. I'll tell them the same thing."

"They are going to be checking cameras."

There is a slight pause before Cameron speaks again. "Cameras? What cameras?"

"In the neighborhood. There may not be any, but they said they were going to check."

"Amelia, I've got to go. I have students coming in. I'm sure it will be fine. And I'm sure no one cut the brake lines. That's just ridiculous. Stop worrying." He hangs up before I can respond.

I walk into the bedroom and open my top dresser drawer. There is no savings account register hidden there. I'm sure I didn't misplace it. I'm sure I don't have one. I shut the dresser drawer and go sit on the couch with my laptop. I haven't had the energy to read Cameron's emails the past few days, but the anger inside of me gives me the strength I need.

. . .

*"Dear Cameron, are you okay? I am so, so sorry that Kenny punched you in the stomach yesterday. He must have followed me to the hotel. I don't know how he found out we would be there. I didn't say a thing to anyone. Did you? We've been careful not to text and I only email from the library on their computers so I really don't know how he found out where I would be unless he's been stalking me. Should I get an order of protection? I just don't know what to do."*

*"Kerri, I'm fine. He's a weakling and didn't hurt me at all. I would have punched him back and taken him down if he hadn't turned and run away. I don't know why you ever married such a dirtbag, but I'm glad you finally got the courage to divorce him. Let's give this a few weeks and then try to meet at the hotel again, shall we? It can be our celebration of freedom from our two crazy ex- and soon to be ex-spouses."*

Funny. Cameron hasn't said anything to me about divorce or even leaving me. I pick up the phone and call Janey.

"Hi, Janey, it's Amelia."

"Hello, sweetie. How are you?"

"Oh, I was in a car accident and cut my head a little."

"No! When was this?"

"A few days ago. I'm okay. Just a few stitches."

"Shall I come take care of you? What do you need, Amelia?"

"Lorna took Rowan while I'm recovering. That's actually a big help. I've been kind of out of it."

"So, what happened? Someone pull out in front of you?"

"No. I was on the Parkway and couldn't slow down or stop until I ran into another vehicle. The police think someone cut the brake lines in my car."

She's quiet, processing that information. "Cameron?" she asks.

"Of course not," I say. *Maybe,* I'm thinking. "Why would he do that?"

"To be rid of you," she says bluntly.

"But Rowan was in the car. He would never hurt Rowan."

"Really?"

I can't answer that truthfully. I don't want to think about it.

"Who else had access to your car?" Janey is like a dog with a bone. She won't stop.

"I don't know. Maybe some teenagers in the neighborhood or something. Cameron thinks the police are wrong, that the lines were just old and worn out."

"Amelia. Think about it. He tried to kill you once before and couldn't do it himself. This would be the perfect way to kill you. If you had died in that crash—which you definitely could have going at a high speed—you wouldn't be around to say the brakes didn't work. They would blame it on inattention or something else. He would be the poor widower, claim the life insurance money I'm sure he has on you, and be free to marry Kerri without anyone batting an eye."

"No! I...he..."

Janey waits patiently for me to finish, but I can't. She's right. I see it all in a flash, clear as day. I can't hide from the truth anymore. A crystal clear thought forms in my mind and, for the first time in a long while, I am not afraid.

"So, will you tell the police?" she asks me.

"No." I am absolutely sure about this. I will not tell the police anything.

"Why not? You're in danger, Amelia."

I'm surprisingly calm. "I have my reasons, Janey. Please don't say anything to anyone."

"I have to!"

"Promise me, Janey. Not one word to anyone. I have a plan. I can't tell you now, but you'll see. Promise me."

She sighs. "I promise, but if anything happens to you, I'm bringing all the evidence we collected to the police."

"Nothing will happen to me. Cameron knows the police are suspicious so he'll be on his best behavior for a while. Long enough for...for me to sort things out here."

Janey doesn't like it, but she agrees and I know she will keep her promise. My head is clearer than it has ever been. I am *outside* myself, not inside anymore. I know exactly what I am going to do.

# Chapter Twenty-Nine

I reach under my side of the bed and remove the envelope of cash I have taped there. For the past three years, I have taken money from Cameron's wallet each week, a dollar here, five dollars there—not enough for him to ever notice, but enough to give me some security. It takes me a few minutes to count it since it is all one dollar and five dollar bills. There is $2,342. I count it again just to be sure. It should be enough.

I put on sweatpants and a sweatshirt, and tie a scarf around my head, tucking in every single strand of hair. I do not put on any makeup, so my skin looks pale and my eyes look slightly sunken. Perfect.

I stop at a thrift shop for a few items, and then drive to New York City in the car Laurence has loaned us. I park in a garage on Lexington Avenue around the corner from Mary's Wig Shop. The bell on the door jingles as I walk in.

"Welcome!" A middle-aged woman greets me with enthusiasm. "How can we help you today?"

I point to my head. "Chemo," I say.

"Oh, don't be embarrassed, my dear. Let's find the

perfect wig for you." She leads me to the back of the store. There are wigs everywhere.

"I am looking for a particular color and style," I tell her. "Short and black, I think. Like that one." I point to a mannequin head sitting on the counter.

"Are you sure? Why not try something bright and color-ful, like this red one?" She picks up a wig and offers it to me.

"I'm pretty sure I want that one." I point to the black wig. "But maybe I'll take another style and color as well, like that long blonde one next to it."

"Okay," she says. "Let's try them on and see how they look."

"Oh, no. I don't want to do that. I'll just try them on at home."

"There are no returns." The woman frowns. "You should definitely try them on to see if you like them."

"Thank you, but I'm too embarrassed. I understand about the returns. How much do I owe you?"

She tells me, and I hand over the cash.

"Thank you," I say.

"You're welcome, dear. Good luck to you. I hope the chemo works."

I just nod and walk out of the shop. Another customer is coming in, and I am relieved to see the saleswoman has forgotten all about me.

There is a Starbucks on the next corner. I ask for the key to the restroom. Since I still look like a cancer patient, they don't hesitate to hand it over. Inside the restroom, I put on makeup and the blonde wig, and change into the jeans and t-shirt I stuffed into my oversized handbag. They are new, purchased from the thrift store on my way here. I add padding to my bra, almost doubling my chest size, and put on a pair of very large sunglasses before I hand the bathroom key over to the person waiting outside the door and leave the store. I give my sweatpants and sweatshirt to a homeless person one block over. They are gray and worn, like a million other pairs in this city, but the woman seems to appreciate them. I am glad I can help her.

I wander over to Times Square and sit on one of the cement posts blocking vehicles from entering the area. I watch for a while until I find what I am looking for.

I take out $500 and move closer to the short man hanging out in the shadows near a building across the street. There have been sketchy-looking people meeting briefly with him one-on-one for about an hour now.

"Hi," I say. I don't even have to pretend to be scared. My hands are shaking. "I need fentanyl. I can pay." I keep my hands in my pockets.

"Go away," he says. "I ain't got nothing."

"Where can I get some? I really, really need it."

"I don't know you. And anyway, that stuff's freaking dangerous." He's looking around nervously. He doesn't want to get caught.

"Please. I'll pay $500 for it."

He looks surprised. "You need it that bad, huh?"

"Yeah. I do."

"Okay. Okay. Let me see the money."

"No. Let me see the fentanyl first."

He reaches into a pocket and pulls out a packet of white powder double-wrapped in a clear plastic baggie. "Here. I hope you know what you're doing. I ain't responsible if you dies."

I take the baggie and stuff it in my pocket. He holds out a hand and I give him the $500.

"Thanks," I say.

"Thanks yourself, blondie," he says, moving away from

me. There is a policeman on his way over to us. The dealer is not sticking around, just in case.

I don't know what to do, so I stand there looking up at the buildings like I'm a tourist. I take out my phone and snap a few pictures.

"Are you alright, miss?" the policeman asks me.

"Oh, yes, sir. I'm fine. Isn't this a wonderful city?" I use my best southern accent. "I've just arrived from Wimberley, Texas. Do y'all know it? It's an itty bitty place, so I'm finding this city a might bit overwhelming. That gentleman —" I wave in the general direction the drug dealer went, "— did not know how I can get to the 9-11 memorial, but maybe y'all can tell me? I sure would appreciate that. I want to pay my respects to those heroes, like y'all are. Thank you so much for protecting us. It sure is an honor to meet y'all."

The policeman relaxes. "Of course." He rattles off directions, and I pretend to listen with great interest. I snap a few more pictures. He gets a call on his radio and rushes off.

I walk back to my car, take off the wig, and change into my own clothes. I put the thrift store clothes in a plastic bag and add it to the pile of garbage on the street before heading home. I'll keep the wig for now, just in case.

# Chapter Thirty

When I get home, I wrap the fentanyl in Christmas paper and then put it in another sealed baggie. I hide it in a tampon box and put it on the top shelf of my closet with the other feminine products I keep there. If Cameron finds it before I can use it, it will ruin everything.

I rummage through Cameron's dresser drawers and find what I am looking for. He's an idiot to keep anything hidden there. It's a note on perfumed purple paper from Kerri that I'm sure he has read over and over again. She has flowery handwriting and dots her i's with little hearts.

*"Dear Cameron,"* it says, *"I can't bear to live without you. I'm so sorry for everything I have put you through this past year. Let's end this and get together soon. Love, Kerri."*

I carefully erase the part that says, "and get," and draw dashes so it now reads "Let's end this—together—soon." I hide the note with the fentanyl. Cameron won't ask me about it even if he notices it is gone. It's too incriminating for him.

It's almost dinner time and Cameron will be home soon,

so I wash my hands and make a chicken casserole. Cameron likes it, and I haven't made it in a while. His mother gave me the recipe. She wanted to help me out. At least, that's what she told me. I think she just didn't like the way mine tasted, although there are only one or two small differences between her recipe and mine.

Cameron comes in the door and gives me a kiss. "How are you feeling?"

"I'm a little better today," I say. "Being able to rest all day without having to work or take care of Rowan helps a lot." I hope he is not monitoring my odometer.

Cameron grunts in reply. He seems distracted.

"How was your day?" I ask.

"Great," he says.

"Good," I say, pulling the casserole from the oven. Cameron sits down at the table and picks at it with his fork. We eat in silence.

"I signed up for a conference this weekend. It's local, but I'm going to stay at the hotel anyway. I'll miss a lot if I'm not there the whole time."

"Okay," I say. "Which hotel?"

"The Hilton. It's the only one with conference facilities and large enough to house all of the attendees."

"Oh, that's nice," I say. "I'm hoping to pick Rowan up from your parents' house this weekend, so I'll be busy getting him settled back home anyway."

Cameron looks relieved that I am not arguing with him. "Okay, then," he says. "I'll pack my stuff tonight and then head to the hotel tomorrow after school."

I pick up the dishes and take them to the sink. "Sounds good," I say. "Will Kerri be going, too?"

Cameron suddenly slams his hand on the table. "Stop it, Amelia. We were having a nice conversation, and you have to bring your jealousy into it. Of course, she's going. All the teachers from the school are going. Geez, Amelia. There's nothing going on here except your craziness. You're imagining things that are insane and totally untrue."

"I'm sorry," I say, not looking at him. I'm not falling for it this time. I know exactly what is going on. I'm not crazy. At least, not anymore.

Cameron takes his beer and goes into the living room to watch television. I clean up the kitchen. "I'm going to bed," I tell him. "I'm not feeling well."

"Sure," he says. "Good night."

I don't know how long he stays up, but I hear him talking on the phone. "I'll bring some wine," I hear him say.

There's a silence on his end for a minute, so I know she's talking.

"You just bring your sexiest lingerie," he says. "We don't have to go to every workshop. We can enjoy ourselves." He laughs quietly. "Yes, of course I've asked Amelia for a divorce. She's agreed. She's not happy either."

I put the pillow over my ears and press tightly. I don't want to hear any more of his lies. He does it so well, so effortlessly. If he ever really asked for a divorce, I would say no just to spite him. He promised to love, honor, and cherish *me*. I should make him do that, not give him an out.

Cameron is gone when I wake up in the morning. He has packed his overnight bag and left the clothes he did not take on the floor of the bedroom. I pick them up and put them back in his drawers. I count the condoms he keeps in the bedside table. Last night, there were fifteen. Today there are ten. The bottle of wine I was saving for him is gone, too.

I sit down at his computer and log in with his credentials. I type an email to Kerri.

. . .

*"Dear Kerri, I am not divorcing Amelia. I lied to you about that. I lied to you about everything just to get you into bed with me. Now that we have been together in that way, I no longer want anything to do with you. I've lost all respect for you. Amelia is my one true love and I want to be with her forever. We are finished. I would like to see you in person, though, just so we can talk about it and you can have closure.*
*—Cameron"*

I schedule it to be sent automatically right after their workday is over. I don't really want either of them to see it. It's just satisfying to write it. I log off.

Around noon, I get dressed in an outfit that's very close to one I've seen Kerri wear and put on the black wig. I use a deep brown eyeliner pencil to make my eyebrows look heavy and bushy and give my face a little bit of a tan with makeup several shades darker than I usually wear. I add a few red blotchy spots and blend them in. I look almost like her. I stuff some extra clothing underneath what I am wearing so I look a little more plump. Perfect. I'll need those clothes anyway. I put the blonde wig, the purple note, and the fentanyl in an old purse I picked up at the thrift store and head out.

There is a liquor store near Kerri's house. I stop there and buy another bottle of Cameron's favorite wine using his credit card. I took it from his wallet this morning. No worries, though. I will put it back today.

I park two blocks away from the Hilton and check my watch. It is 1:45 pm. I walk briskly to the hotel and tell the man behind the desk that I have a reservation. "My name is Kerri Jacquet, or it might be under Kerri Dallas. We're newly married," I say, looking down in a way that I hope he interprets as shyness.

"Ah, yes. A reservation for two. Your husband has already checked you in. Here is your key." He hands me a small envelope.

"Oh! Is he in the room? I wanted to surprise him." I keep my voice low and husky.

"I think he left a moment ago. You just missed him."

"Thank you very much," I say, keeping my head low and tilted away from the security cameras.

I take the key and use it to open room 521. Cameron has definitely been there. His overnight bag is open on the floor. He has put the wine he took from the house in a bucket of ice and spread rose petals on the bed. I put on a pair of medical grade gloves. According to all of the crime shows I have seen, it is important to leave no fingerprints. I hide the purple note and his credit card inside his bag, and take the packet of fentanyl out of my purse. My hands are shaking. I try to pop the cork on the wine I have brought, but my hands are shaking so much I cannot do it. I start to cry. I am a failure at everything. I can't even put poison into a wine bottle. I sprinkle the fentanyl over the strawberries that are sitting in a dish next to the wine. It looks like powdered sugar.

I don't dare stay any longer. I don't know when Cameron will be back. I put the extra bottle of wine back in my bag and throw the fentanyl packet under the bed, making sure a corner of the plastic bag peeks out just a little so that it's hidden from Cameron and Kerri, but will not be hard to find when the police are looking for it. Maybe he'll go to jail after I call in an anonymous tip. I can at least do that.

I walk back to the lobby and go into the public restroom,

locking the door behind me. I wash my face and change out of the drab clothes into the more form fitting ones I had rolled up and stuffed underneath them. I put on another set of thrift store clothes over the top of those, just to be safe. I put on the blonde wig and a baseball cap, adjust it so that my face is partially hidden, then unlock the door and exit the restroom.

I hear Cameron's voice before I see him. I duck behind a pillar.

"I came early to have everything ready for us," he says. "You don't need to stop at the desk. No one will ever know you are staying in my room."

"You think of everything, Cameron." Kerri's husky voice is unmistakable.

The voices drift off as they walk toward the elevator and get on.

I hurry out the door and arrive back at my car, breathless. I take off the wig, brush my hair, put on some lipstick, and pull off the thrift store clothes I have been wearing over my own clothes. I look like myself again. There's a Goodwill near me. I think about driving there and dumping the old clothes and the wigs into their donation bin, but change my mind. The police might look there. Eric and Lyla are away this weekend—I heard them telling Cameron they were going on a cruise. So, I take the clothes and the purse to their house instead and burn them in their backyard fire pit. I know they have a front door camera, so I am careful to park down the street and enter and exit their backyard through their neighbor's backyard. He's an old man with poor eyesight who knows absolutely nothing about cameras or technology and who rarely gets up from his chair in front of the television. I don't think he saw me.

# Chapter Thirty-One

Rowan is home with me again. I picked him up after I left Eric and Lyla's house. He's happy to see me and won't leave my side. He follows me everywhere and cries if I shut the bathroom door behind me. He's still little, so it's okay. I let him watch me sit on the toilet. Maybe he'll want to try this himself soon. I have been a little neglectful in potty-training. He's two. It's probably time. It will be nice not to have to change diapers.

It's been a couple of days since Cameron left. "It's quiet without Cameron around," I tell Janey this morning. She calls me every day at 10:00. "I haven't heard from him since he left for his conference. He must be having a good time."

"You'd think he'd at least check in with you," she says. I can hear the scowl in her voice.

"Well, that's Cameron," I say. "He gets so involved in something that he forgets everything else."

"Still..." Her voice trails off and I know she is thinking about his affair with Kerri.

"It's not Kerri," I say. "He told me he broke that off and

that he loves only me. Our marriage has been really, really good lately."

"Are you sure about that?" Janey is very skeptical. I have to convince her.

"Absolutely," I say. "We may even have another baby soon if things keep going so well." I giggle. "It's like when we were first married. He dotes on me, brings me flowers—" I make a mental note to pick up some flowers from the grocery store—old ones so it will look like they've been here a few days.

"Okay, then," she says. "I'm glad you're happy."

"I am, Janey. Very happy. I think it's fine for you to shred all those emails we printed out now."

"How's Rowan?" she asks. I don't push it. I don't want her to get suspicious.

"He's great. We're working on potty training." I tell her some funny stories about Rowan and my inexperience with little boys. "I think he's getting the hang of it, though. His aim is improving."

Janey laughs. She knows. She raised a son.

The doorbell rings. "I've got to go, Janey. Someone's at the door," I say.

"Okay. Talk to you tomorrow," she says. I hope that will be true. I see the police car parked out front.

"Hello," I say to the two policemen standing on my front porch. "How can I help you?"

"Are you Mrs. Dallas?" the older of the two asks. He's a little overweight and has gray hair near his temples. The rest of his hair is jet black and cut short. His face is kind, though, and he is looking at me with concern and sympathy. The younger one has a crew cut, like he's fresh out of the academy. He is so skinny, I am not sure how he would win in any fight with a criminal. He looks like he could be crushed in seconds. He shifts his weight nervously from foot to foot, not looking at me at all.

"I am Amelia Dallas, yes," I say.

"May we come in?" the older officer asks. His name tag says "Officer Smith." Well, that will be easy to remember. I can't quite see the younger officer's name tag. He's standing too far away.

"What is this about?" I ask. I bend down to pick up Rowan. He's been hanging on my leg, hiding behind me.

"It's about your husband, ma'am," Officer Smith says. "I'm afraid we have bad news."

"Oh," I say, trying to sound worried. "Come in. Can I get you something to drink? Coffee? Water?"

"No, thank you." Officer Smith speaks for both of them. The younger one still isn't looking at me, but I can see his nametag now: Officer Kachinski.

I lead them to the living room. They sit on the couch. I sit in a chair with Rowan on my lap. He's clinging to my neck. I don't think he likes these men much.

"What is it?" I say. "Is he okay?"

"I'm afraid not," says Officer Smith. "He was found dead at the Hilton this morning."

I gasp. "What? That can't be right. You must have the wrong person."

Officer Smith holds out Cameron's driver's license. "Is this your husband?"

I take the license and stare at it. "Yes," I whisper.

"Did you know he was at the hotel?" Officer Smith asks me.

"Yes. Yes. He was there for a conference." I speak softly and slowly, with my head down. "What...what happened?" I lift my head. There are tears in my eyes. Officer Smith reaches over and pats my knee.

"Do you know a woman named Kerri Jacquet?" Officer Kachinski asks, taking out a small notebook and pen.

I stare at him. "Yes," I say as if I am wondering why he is asking this. "She works with Cameron. She's...she's a friend of ours."

"Is that right." It's a comment, not a question. "I see." I can hear the sarcasm in his voice.

I say nothing. Rowan fidgets on my lap. I put him down and he toddles away to play with his toys in his room. He's bored now. I feel a little prick of excitement in my chest, but I keep my face blank.

"I don't understand," I say.

"I am so sorry." Officer Smith appears to be really concerned for me. He thinks I've just lost someone who is important to me. "We think they may have been having an affair," he continues.

"No. No, that can't be right," I say. "Why would you even think that? Cameron was a devoted husband and father. He would never do that."

"There is evidence. I can't share everything with you right now, but we have been pretty thorough in our investigation. We believe that Cameron was trying to break things off, but Kerri wasn't willing to let him go, so there was a struggle and she killed him and then, possibly, killed herself. Or, it may be that your husband killed her in self-defense, but it was too late. They both bled to death."

I am silent for a minute. This is not what I was expecting. Surely, they meant death by eating strawberries laced with fentanyl, not bleeding out. Are they trying to trick me? Are they hoping I will ask about the poison so they can force a confession? *"Ah ha!"* they will say. *"And how did you know that, Mrs. Dallas?"*

They are obviously waiting for me to say *something*, so eventually, I look up and ask, "How?"

"We can't say while the investigation is still ongoing."

"No, I mean, how would it be possible for Kerri to do such a thing? She's smaller. He could have stopped her from attacking him in any way. Besides, she was nice. She would never do such a thing."

The policemen exchange glances. "We're pretty sure about this. I am so sorry."

"Can I see him? My husband? Where is he?"

"Actually, we do need you to come to the morgue to identify the body. Do you think you would be up to doing that?"

I nod and choke back a sob. It's a real one. It surprises me.

They leave, and I pick up my phone to call Lorna. But first, I call Cameron's number. He doesn't answer, of course. It goes straight to voice mail. "Cameron, the police were here. They think you're...dead. Please call me. I can't believe you're gone. Please, please call me and let me know you are alright."

Next, I dial Lorna. "Lorna, something awful has happened. The police were just here, and they said...they said..."

"What is it, Amelia?" Lorna can hear the panic in my voice. "Oh my God, is it Cameron? What's happened to Cameron?"

"He's...he's dead, Lorna. The police say he was murdered."

Lorna wails and I have to hold the phone away from my ear for a minute. "No! No! Not my son! No! Who did this? What happened? May they be damned to hell!"

"He was at a conference at the Hilton. The police said

Kerri—a woman who works with him—was angry that he wouldn't accept her romantic advances, and that she killed him."

"That's ludicrous." She's still sniffling, but she's calmed down a bit. "He would never lead anyone on like that or be unkind. The police have that part wrong."

"That's what I said. They want me to go to the morgue to identify the body. Will you come with me?"

"Of course. Laurence and I will meet you there? Can you get someone to watch Rowan? He should not see his father like this." She starts to wail again.

"I don't have a babysitter. I was hoping Laurence—"

"No. Laurence will want to see his son. Figure something else out. I'll see you in twenty minutes." She hangs up abruptly, like she's blaming me for this.

It takes me a minute, but then I call Lyla. "Can you watch Rowan this morning? I have to go to the—morgue."

"What?" Lyla sounds a bit distracted. "Just a minute, Amelia. Julia! Julia! Stop jumping on the couch!" she shouts at her daughter. I hold the phone away from my ear. "Sorry, Amelia. Julia is a handful. Can I call you back?"

"Cameron is dead."

There is silence, so I continue, hoping she hasn't hung up yet.

"I can't call you back, Lyla. I have to go to the morgue to identify Cameron's body. I need someone to watch Rowan while I do that."

"Oh my god, Amelia. What happened?"

"I'm not sure yet. The police think he might have been murdered." I sound calm. "Can you...can you please watch Rowan?"

"Of course! I'm so sorry for you, Amelia. I don't know what to say."

"Thanks." I clear my throat. "I'll be there in about ten minutes."

I hang up and pack several diapers, snacks, and toys for Rowan. I don't know how long I will be. It could be a very long time.

After I drop Rowan off, I call Janey.

"What's wrong?" She knows immediately that something bad has happened. I never call her at this time of day.

"Cameron is dead," I say. "It was two policemen ringing my doorbell this morning. They came to tell me. I'm on my way to the morgue now."

"What happened?" Janey's voice is quiet. I think she knows.

"The policemen think Kerri killed him," I tell her.

"Why do they think that?" She seems concerned. Worried.

"They found Cameron dead in a hotel room."

"Okay," she says. "But why do they think Kerri killed him?"

"There was a note," I say. "And an email."

"Hmm," Janey says. I imagine her furrowed brow and frown as she tries to make sense of this. "I'm coming there. You'll need me."

"Thanks," I say. "But will you please destroy the emails you printed first?"

"I'll be there soon," she says. "See you tonight."

"Janey, please—" I start to say, but she has already hung up.

I've arrived at the morgue. I follow the signs to the back of the hospital where there is a teeny tiny sign on the corner of the building that says "Morgue Entrance," with steps leading down some stairs to a double steel door, so I guess I am in the right place. I pull into a parking spot marked for visitors. Who else comes to a morgue? You're either the dead person, who wouldn't need a parking spot, or a visitor. It seems silly to me to mark the parking spots that way. I rub my eyes to make them red, throw my phone in my purse, and get out of the car.

I've never been to a morgue. I pick up the phone hanging on the wall to the left of the door. It rings five times before someone answers.

"I'm Amelia Dallas," I say. "Officer Smith told me to come—to identify my husband's body." The door buzzes and unlocks. I open it and walk in. It's cold, and there's a peculiar odor that I really don't like. A short, stocky lady with grey curly hair and large black glasses walks toward me.

"I'm Dr. Arzt, the coroner," she says. Her voice sounds gravelly and a bit hoarse, like she hasn't spoken in days. "Usually a police officer comes with the relative. I didn't expect you to come on your own."

"Oh," I say.

"Wait here," she says, pointing to a worn couch in the hallway. "I'll call him. Officer Smith, you said?"

I nod and sit. She's gone for sixteen minutes. I know, because I have been staring at my watch. The outside door buzzes and clicks. Officer Smith comes in with Lorna and Laurence.

"Amelia," he says. "We were waiting for you at the station."

"I'm sorry. I didn't know," I say. I keep my head down and my hands folded in my lap so I don't have to look at Lorna or Laurence.

"Of course not," says Officer Smith apologetically. "It's not a problem. It's just that we want to be with you to offer support."

I don't answer.

"We're all devastated," Lorna says, coming over to sit beside me. She puts her arm around my shoulders. I hug her and choke back a sob. I'm good at this.

Laurence sits on the other side of me and puts his arms around us both. I can see that he had been crying and hugging me has opened the floodgates again. He is fighting for breath between sobs. Now I really do feel badly. Cameron was their oldest son, the heir apparent. I can't imagine losing Rowan the way they have lost Cameron. Thinking about that makes the tears come for real.

Dr. Arzt comes back. "Are we ready?" she asks Officer Smith.

He looks at me, and I nod. Lorna hands me a tissue, and I dab at my eyes. Laurence blows his nose on a cotton hand-kerchief with his initials in the corner and puts it back in his pocket. They misinterpret my silence as reluctance to be here, to be doing what we have to do next. Lorna takes my hand, and we walk into a clean, sterile, room where Cameron is lying on an aluminum table. Kerri is lying on another table next to him. At least, I think it is them. Both bodies are entirely covered with white sheets.

Dr. Arzt pulls back the sheet on the first body. It is definitely Cameron. He looks a little different, pale and waxy, but I nod to Officer Smith and turn my head away. It really is a shock to see him this way. I lean against the table and feel the bruise on my hip where Cameron kicked me a week ago. He said it was an accident, that he had a bad dream and kicked out in his sleep, but I know better. He was angry because I was reading and wouldn't turn the light off so he could sleep. Actually, I think he was angry because he wanted *me* to go to sleep so he could text Kerri. It doesn't matter anymore. I try not to let my face show my indifference. I don't want Officer Smith asking questions. Instead, I lean over and kiss Cameron's forehead. It's cold.

"Don't touch him!" Dr. Arzt says, pulling me away. "I haven't done the autopsy yet."

"Autopsy?" Lorna asks. "You'll be cutting my boy open? No. No! I refuse to allow that."

"Actually, since we think this was a murder, we have to do one," Officer Smith says. "I'm so sorry."

I wish he would stop saying that. He's not any sorrier than I am. I'm sure he sees this type of thing a lot. He's a cop.

"Is that Kerri?" I point to the other table.

Neither Officer Smith or Dr. Arzt answers right away, but I can see by their faces that it is.

"We are waiting for her husband to arrive to identify the body," Officer Smith finally says.

I forgot about that. I hope he doesn't say anything to Officer Smith about talking to me about the affair. If he does, I can deny it. Knowing about the affair will make him a suspect, though, so if he's smart, he'll keep his mouth shut.

He doesn't. He comes in as we are leaving. There are no tears in his eyes. He winks at me. Before the door closes behind us, I hear him say, "Yes, that's Kerri. Slut. She got what she deserved."

# Chapter Thirty-Two

It's been two weeks since I've heard from Officer Smith. Lorna calls me every day to ask if I know anything more. I'm just as much in the dark as she is. I really have no idea what the police found from the autopsy or the investigation, or what they are thinking *really* happened.

We've buried Cameron in his family plot—Laurence and Lorna insisted. I allowed them to take over all of the arrangements. He was their son, after all. They should remember him the way they want to. I tell them I can't possibly speak at the funeral. It's too much. I'm overwhelmed with sorrow. Yada yada yada.

Janey has been staying with me. She doesn't say much—just watches me, makes dinner, cleans the house, and helps with Rowan. We don't speak about any of it. I play the part of a grieving widow convincingly so she doesn't push me. I cannot tell even Janey what the truth really is. She might accidentally give me away. She wouldn't do it on purpose, but the cops can be tricky when they ask you questions. I know that from when I was questioned about my mother.

They made me say things that were not true and convinced me that I was guilty when I wasn't. I know I wasn't. I would never, ever have hurt my mother. My father did that. But the police wouldn't listen. "He has an airtight alibi," they said. "He was on the phone with a friend when it happened. We have the phone records. We have statements. There is no way he could have done it. You're lying, Amelia. Stop lying. Just tell us the truth."

I'm not surprised when Officer Smith calls to ask me to come down to the station to answer a few questions.

"Of course," I say. "Janey is here to look after Rowan so I can come right away."

He keeps me waiting when I get there. That's what they always do. Keep you waiting, get you nervous, so you'll say anything they want you to say.

"How are you doing, Amelia?" Officer Smith looks like he really cares. I know better.

"It's difficult," I say. "Rowan asks for his daddy and I don't know what to tell him. That just makes me miss Cameron all the more. It's not fair."

"We want to wrap this up as quickly as possible to give you closure," he says, patting my hand. "I just have a few questions for you."

"Okay," I say, wiping my eyes with the tissue I hold tightly in my right hand.

"Did you know Cameron was having an affair with Kerri?"

"No. No. He wouldn't do that," I say. "Why would you say that?" I am the perfect model of an innocent, naive wife.

"They were together in the hotel room, both of them, um, un-dressed."

I look down and fold my hands in my lap.

"Did you ever have a conversation with Kerri's husband, Kenneth?"

"Of course. Kenny and Kerri were friends of ours."

"I mean—about Cameron and Kerri having an affair."

I pause. I need to be careful. I need to tell the truth, at least some of it.

"Yes, Kenny called me once to accuse Cameron, but I know it was a lie. I think he may have been drunk when he called me."

"I don't think it was a lie, Amelia." Officer Smith sounds sympathetic. "Cameron and Kerri were together in the hotel room."

A tear rolls down my cheek. I don't wipe it away.

"You didn't suspect anything between them?" Officer Smith asks.

"No. Cameron was a perfect husband and father. He loved me, and I loved him." If I answer any other way, he might put me on his list of suspects. I am okay with Kenny being on that list. A jealous husband kills his wife and her lover. That works just as well as Kerri killing Cameron because he rejected her. Either way is fine with me.

Officer Smith shakes his head. He doesn't think he's getting through to me. Obviously, if Cameron was having an affair, he was not a perfect husband and father. He looks at me for a minute, then asks another question.

"Did Cameron or Kerri have any enemies?"

"Oh my! No!" I look at him with wide eyes as if I'm shocked at the question. "Kerri was really sweet and Cameron was loved by everyone. He is—was—so popular. He would do anything for you." I pull a Kleenex from the box in the center of the table and wipe my eyes. "Do you know who...killed him?" I blow my nose as daintily as I can.

Officer Smith hesitates. "We have two theories at this

point, but I can't share them with you. It's an ongoing investigation. Once we make an arrest, I can give you more information."

"Thank you," I say.

"Did you know about any emails between your husband and Kerri?"

That one throws me off-balance and I don't answer right away.

"Mrs. Dallas?" Officer Smith reaches across the table and puts his hand over my hand. "Did you know about any emails between your husband and Kerri?"

"There may have been a few. They worked together." I sound defensive, but inside I am panicking.

"What about other online activities? Did your husband engage in any sexual conversations with women online?"

"No! Of course not."

"Well, someone printed copies of conversations of a sexual nature your husband had with multiple other women and gave them to Kerri's husband. We believe that he shared those with Kerri and that might be what set her off."

I am actually shocked now, and it shows on my face. What Officer Smith does not know is that I am not shocked at what he has told me. I am shocked that someone sent copies to Kerri. Someone I trusted. Someone I thought had shredded them. Someone who has helped destroy a monster. I am grateful, but hope the police don't pin it on me. I wonder if they can tell where the copies were printed.

"Who would do that?" I let a tear roll down my cheek and makes sure he sees it before I wipe it away. "Who would make something like that up and then spread it around? Do you think it was Kerri's husband? He *was* convinced they were having an affair. He's ruined my life with his stupid jealousy!" I put my head down on the table and sob. Officer Smith lets me cry for a few minutes before tentatively patting my back and offering me a tissue.

"We do know Kenny received, uh, other information, that might have caused him to become angry. I'm sorry. I can't say anything more." Officer Smith stands up and offers me his hand. I take it and stand shakily to my feet. "That's all the questions I have for you right now. Will you be alright driving home?"

"Yes. Yes, I think so," I say. "It's not far. I'm going to pick up my son first, though. What do I tell him, Officer Smith? What do I tell him about his daddy?" I use the Kleenex to wipe my nose again.

"Here's the contact information for a therapist." He hands me a business card but I can't really make out the name or number on it. "She can help you with that."

"Thank you."

Officer Smith shows me the way out, and I head back to my car. The giggles come without warning. I can't stop them. I cover my eyes and put my head down. Anyone watching will think I'm sobbing with grief. But I'm not. I'm laughing. I feel so...free.

# Chapter Thirty-Three

They haven't arrested Kenny. I've been watching the news every night. The day after the murders were discovered, it was on every station. Now, a month later, no one is talking about it. For the first time in a long time, I have no bruises anywhere on my body. Janey has gone home, and I am back in a routine that makes me happy. Work for me. Daycare for Rowan. He doesn't ask about his daddy anymore. Toddlers are so adaptable that way.

I've just put him to bed and am sitting down to watch television with my nightly cup of tea when the doorbell rings.

Officer Smith is standing there. He's alone. That's good. I think they always bring two officers if they are coming to arrest you.

"I'm sorry to stop by so late, but I thought you should know before it hits the news tomorrow morning."

"Come in," I say. "Can I get you a cup of coffee? Tea?"

"Yes," he says, surprising me. "Thank you. That would be nice. Coffee. Decaf, if you have it."

He follows me into the kitchen and sits at the table while I make the coffee and serve it to him in a plain white mug. My tea is lukewarm now, but I sit across from him and sip it anyway.

"We've closed the case," he says.

"So, can you tell me what happened now?" I put my teacup down.

"Yes. It will all be on the news tomorrow morning, so there's nothing to hide anymore," he says.

I wait. He sighs and takes a sip of his coffee before continuing.

"We believe Kenneth Jacquet was given a packet of information about your husband from an unidentified source that included emails between your husband and Kerri. Mr. Jacquet swears it wasn't you. He described the person who handed him the packet as an old woman with a German accent. This woman told him her granddaughter was one of the girls Cameron was talking to on a sex chat site. This girl is a computer analyst, and she managed to find out all the other things he was doing. We were not able to confirm that, since we couldn't find the old woman or her granddaughter, but my tech advisors say it is rather easy to hack into someone's computer if you know what you're doing, so we took Mr. Jacquet at his word on this one."

"Oh," I say.

"Mr. Jacquet says he shared the information with his wife to show her that Cameron wasn't the knight in shining armor she thought he was. I'm so sorry, Amelia."

"Oh," I say again, blinking back tears. "So, he was—he did—do those things?"

"Yes," Officer Smith says. "He deceived you, my dear. Do you want me to go on? We can wait a bit if it's too much."

"Oh, no. Please. I need to hear the whole thing," I say. My voice breaks as if I am struggling to control my emotions.

"Well, after Mr. Jacquet shared these with his wife, she got angry and stormed out. He did not know where she was going. That was the night, uh—" Officer Smith checks his notes. "Yes, that was the night she met him at the hotel. The hotel clerk confirms that a Kerri Jacquet matching her description checked in as Kerri Dallas. He says she took a key and went up to the room to wait for her husband—at least that's what she told him. She was going to surprise him. We see her on the hotel cameras going into the room alone, then coming out, then re-entering a little while later with Cameron."

I nod. I'm not crying, so Officer Smith continues.

"We found a plastic bag containing a white powder residue very similar to fentanyl under the bed. She was evidently planning on poisoning him. That's actually what confirmed for us that it was Kerri who did the killing. Women use poison, you know." Officer Smith seems proud to have that knowledge. Everyone who watches any crime TV show knows that, though.

"What Kerri did not realize was that it was not fentanyl in the bag. Someone had sold her a sedative so the drug she sprinkled on the strawberries would never have killed Cameron, but it did make him slow and drowsy."

"Oh my!" I say. I am angry at the person who sold me the fentanyl, but I don't dare show any of that. Hopefully, Officer Smith will just think I'm upset about what he's telling me.

"Cameron had his hands and feet tied to the bed. We believe Kerri lured him into that position after reading about his fantasies about doing just that with the, uh, the

240

other women online. Once he was helpless, she stabbed him in the—in the—pelvic area and cut off—cut off his— well, you know. She managed a few more stabs to his abdomen. He was able to get his hands free and grab her by the hair, pulling her toward him. Cameron took the knife from Kerri and stabbed her through the heart. She fell on top of him and he was not able to get out from under her so they lay there for—" Officer Smith checks his notes again. "For thirty-six to forty-eight hours. Kerri died almost instantly, but Cameron most likely took several hours to bleed out. I'm so sorry. Are you alright?" Officer Smith looks up from his notes and adjusts his glasses.

"No," I say, but I really *am* fine. I am more than fine. I am happy that Cameron had to endure hours of pain. It serves him right. I actually like Kerri at this moment. She did what I was unable to do, what I failed to do. I want to laugh. I want to dance. But, I put on a somber face instead.

"Thank you for telling me, though, Officer Smith," I say. "I needed to know."

He clears his throat. "Well, uh, anyway, the case is closed and we've informed the media. Do you have someone to stay with you tomorrow? The press may show up at your door to ask you questions. Or, you might get curiosity seekers who want to take pictures of your house or you or both."

"I'll be fine," I say. "Thank you."

"Okay, then." Officer Smith stands up and reaches out to shake my hand. "Good luck and let me know if you need any backup tomorrow. I'm so sorry this happened to you."

I take his hand and shake it weakly. "I appreciate your concern for us, Officer Smith," I tell him. "It will take a while for it all to sink in, I think."

He nods at me and walks to the door. "Goodbye, then," he says.

"Goodbye." I shut the door behind him and pull out my phone. Janey answers immediately. I think she's been waiting for me to call. I tell her everything that Officer Smith has just told me. We are both doubled over in laughter by the end of the conversation.

"Vielen Dank, mein Freund," I say.

This sends Janey off on another bout of laughter. "Gern geschehen. Es war mir eine Freude. A pleasure. Truly, a pleasure."

# Chapter Thirty-Four

I'm standing in my hallway next to a suitcase, wearing a tan woolen coat and gloves. The house is empty and every sound I make echoes in the air around me. I walk into the living room for one final inspection and stop to look out the front window. Squirrels scamper up and down the trees. Birds fly by on their way to a warmer climate. A passerby would never know that anything had ever been amiss here. It's peaceful. It's normal.

Lorna and Laurence were the first to move away. They could not stand the embarrassment of the details of their son's murder being shown on national television. Strangers whispered behind their backs at the grocery store. Their friends fell away one by one, unwilling to be associated with the people who had raised such a perverted man.

Lyla and Eric can't look at me. I think they still support Cameron. They are loyal friends to him. It doesn't matter. They were never *my* friends. I hope they are enjoying their fire pit as much as I did. I always wave to their elderly neighbor when I drive by now. I've seen him wink at me once or twice like he *knows* and approves.

I have no idea what has happened to Kenny. I don't really care to know. He was just as much a monster as Cameron was, I think. I pray for justice for him as well. Who knows when that will come or what that will look like...

I take a deep breath. Janey and Rowan are waiting for me in the car, but I can't seem to let go of this life. I know I need to move, to start fresh, to make better memories, but something holds me back. It is extremely difficult for me to love anyone, and yet I did love once. I loved Cameron completely, entrusted him with my whole self, body and soul. I believed he loved me back. Now, he will never love me back. It's too late.

Before I turn away from the window, I see a car I recognize driving slowly down the street. It's Kerri's car. My phone rings.

I forget to check the caller ID and answer without thinking. "Hello?"

"You're welcome," a male voice says into my ear.

"Kenny?" I say.

He laughs and hangs up. The car turns the corner goes out of sight. I don't think anyone in this town will see him again. I think he is moving as far away as I am. I will be happy in Maine. I hope he will be happy wherever he is going.

"Goodbye," I say out loud to no one in particular, picking up my suitcase. I shut the door behind me, making sure it is locked before I get in the car with Janey and Rowan.

"I'm ready," I say.

"Great," Janey says. "Let's go."

She drives in silence, giving me sideways glances every now and then.

"Good?" she asks when we are finally on the highway.
"Very good," I say, smiling.